THE RIVER MOTOR BOAT
BOYS ON THE MISSISSIPPI

HARRY GORDON

THE SIX RIVER MOTOR BOYS ON THE MISSISSIPPI

CHAPTER I — A RAMBLER RECEPTION DAY

A white bulldog of ferocious aspect lay sound asleep under a small table. Lying across the dog's neck, with his soft muzzle hidden between capable paws, was a quarter-grown grizzly bear. Now and then Captain Joe, as the dog was named, stirred uneasily in his sleep, as if in remonstrance at the liberties which Teddy, the cub, was taking with his person. The bulldog and the cub snored in unison!

The table under which the animals slept stood in the middle of the small cabin of the motor boat Rambler, and the Rambler was pulling at her anchor chain in the muddy water of the Mississippi river — pulling and jerking for all the world like a fat pig with a ring in his nose trying to get rid of the line which held him in captivity.

Although early in November, there were wandering flakes of snow in the air, and a chill wind from the northwest was sweeping over the Mississippi valley. There had been several days of continuous rain, and, at Cairo, where the motor boat lay, both the Mississippi and the Ohio rivers were out of their banks.

In spite of the wind and snow, however, the cabin of the Rambler was cozy and warm. In front of the table where the bulldog and the young bear lay stood a coal stove, on the top of which two boys of sixteen, Clayton Emmett and Alexander Smithwick, were cooking ham and eggs, the appetizing flavor of which filled the little room. A dish of sliced potatoes stood not far away, and over the cherry-red coils of an electric stove at the rear of the cabin a great pot of coffee was sizzling and adding its fragrance to rich contributions of the frying pan.

While the boys, growing hungrier every second, stirred the fire and laid the table, footsteps were heard on the forward deck of the motor boat, and then, without even announcing his presence by a knock, a roughly-dressed man of perhaps forty years stepped into the cabin and stood for a moment staring at the bulldog and the bear, stood with a hand on the knob of the door, as if ready for retreat, his lips open, as if the view of the interior had checked words half spoken. Alex. Smithwick regarded the man for a moment with a flash of anger in his eyes, then he caught the humor of the situation and resolved to punish the intruder for his impudence in walking into the cabin without a bit of ceremony.

"Look out for the bulldog and the bear!" he warned. "They consumed two river-men last week! The bulldog tears 'em down, an' the bear eats 'em!"

"What kind of a menagerie is this?" began the visitor, but Alex. gave the bulldog a touch with his foot, and the dog and the bear were in the middle of the space between the table and the stove, snarling fiercely, before the startled intruder could open the door. "Call the brutes off!" he added as Teddy began boxing the empty air.

"Don't stand in the doorway!" Alex. warned, while Clay Emmett turned his face away so as not to betray his enjoyment of the situation. "It makes 'em mad to keep the door open! What do you want?"

The visitor stepped outside and beckoned to the boys through the glass panel. Alex. went out on the deck and stood waiting. The visitor was evidently a riverman, tall, muscular, heavy of hand and sullen of face. He wore rough clothing, neither clean nor whole, and his face was well covered by a bushy beard, light in color except around the mouth, where it was stained with tobacco. Alex. noted that he looked away whenever their eyes met for an instant.

"I'm Gid Brent, the riverman," he said, in a moment, "and I've come to warn you boys against starting out alone, on the river in this boat."

"That's kind of you," Alex. replied. "What's the matter with the boat?"

"It is the river there's something the matter with," replied the other. "The water is high, and is pouring into all the old channels and ditches from Cairo to the Gulf. If you start out without a pilot, you'll run into some bayou and end in a swamp, a couple of hundred miles from the main channel."

"You're a pilot, eh?" asked Alex., with a provoking grin.

"Yes; and I'm called the best on the river," was the boasting reply.

"And you're looking for a job?" Alex. continued, insinuatingly.

"I might accept the right kind of a job," Brent replied, "but I shouldn't want any menagerie on board with me. Where are you boys going?"

"Oh, well," Alex. said, gravely, though there was fun in his eyes, "if you object to our pets, that settles it! We brought Captain Joe, the bulldog, from the Amazon, and Teddy Bear, the cub, from British Columbia."

"Oh, if they're tame!" the other exclaimed. "I might — —"

"I'll call 'em out an' see what they say to you!" Alex. replied, mischief in his eyes, opening the cabin door and inviting the bulldog and the bear out to the deck!

Captain Joe snarled at the man's feet and Teddy Bear stood up and squared off in front of him in a boxing attitude! Brent swung toward the little pier against which the motor boat lay, and the animals, thus encouraged, sprang at him.

In a minute the pilot was on the pier, racing toward the shore as if for his life! Clay came out on deck and both boys stood laughing at the retreating figure. Presently Brent came to an old warehouse, where security might be found in an open doorway. Here he stopped and turned back, shaking a fist at the grinning lads.

"I'll be even with you for that!" he shouted. "I'll teach you to set your dog on me, you miserable little bum-boat tramps! I'll show you!"

"Get him, Captain Joe!" cried Alex., angry at the impertinent language used, but Clay caught the bulldog by the collar and held him back.

"All right!" smiled Alex. "Let the tramp go, if you want to! Anyway, I'm about half starved! Funny, Case and Jule don't get back! They've been gone three hours!"

"They'll get cold beans for supper if they don't show up pretty soon!" Clay said, turning back to the cabin. "The ham and eggs and potatoes are just done!"

Even as Alex. closed the cabin door behind himself, running footsteps were heard, and the next moment two boys of about his own age, Cornelius Witters and Julian Shafer, made their appearance, racing off the pier and on to the deck of the motor boat like young colts. They dashed into the cabin and dropped down into seats at the table.

"What's the matter with the fellow at the head of the pier?" Case Witters asked. "He called to us not to come down here! Said there was a crazy boy, a mad dog and a grizzly loose in the boat! Guess you got him peeved, didn't you?"

"He's too fresh!" Alex. responded. "He came on board as if he owned the boat, and then had the nerve to tell us that we'd get lost if we went down the river without a pilot! He wanted a pilot's job! We should have given Captain Joe a bite out of him!"

"Did he say he was a pilot?" asked Jule Shafer, with a wink at Case.

"Sure thing he did!" answered Alex. "Said he was the best on the river!"

"Well," Case began, "if he is a pilot he is out of practice! I heard him asking a man about the passage from Hickman to Reelfoot lake. When we went up-town that same man who spoke to us on the pier stood on the levee with a bunch of toughs. Their heads were together, as if they were planning mischief. I thought they looked at Jule and I in a strange way, too!"

"I don't believe he ever came on board to get a job!" Jule broke in. "He's a spy! That's just what he is, and I wish Captain Joe had eaten him up!"

"But why should he come spying here?" asked Clay. "We're not river thieves!"

"Well, there's something odd going on at Cairo!" Case asserted. "There are crowds on the streets, and the policemen seem to be on their metal! I guess we would have been locked up as suspects if we hadn't had on pretty good clothes!"

"Why didn't you ask some one to tell you about it?" demanded Alex.

"We did," Jule answered, "and got our trouble for our pains! There's been a warehouse robbery up the river somewhere, but I don't see why that should make such a stir down here at Cairo. The merchant I ordered the gasoline of said that $100,000 in diamonds and furs had been taken, and that a watchman who resisted had been seriously wounded."

"Perhaps they think we're the thieves!" suggested Clay.

"I shouldn't wonder if they did," Case grinned. "Anyway, the men I talked with seemed to have loose shingles — they acted that way, all right!"

"Loose shingles!" cried Alex. "You'll wash dishes for a week for that! Loose shingles is slang, and we're not to talk slang. If you wanted to indicate a slant in the belfry, why didn't you say — —"

"Slant in the belfry!" roared Case. "Guess that isn't slang! I'll have plenty of help washing dishes, all right. S-a-a-y, listen to that, will you!"

As the boy spoke he lifted a hand for silence, and the four sat at the table silent and motionless. It was growing dusk now, and the deck of the motor boat showed dim under the gathering shadows of the night. While the lads sat there, listening, Captain Joe, the bulldog, ran to the closed door and sniffed suspiciously.

"There's some one out on deck!" Case exclaimed, then. "I wonder if that fellow has had the nerve to come back here? I'll go and see who it is, anyway."

"Why don't you wait and see what he will do?" asked Clay. "If he thinks we're the robbers, he'll show himself directly. If it is only a sneak thief, he'll take a jump in the river the minute he knows we are aware of his presence on the deck. Give him a chance!"

Then three words came in a whisper from the outside of the door. They were spoken in a trembling voice, accompanied by a soft knock on the lower panel.

"Let me in!" the voice said. It seemed like the voice of a child, too.

"Come on in, if you want to!" Alex. answered. "This seems to be our reception day!"

"Sure! Come on in! Don't be so mysterious about it, whoever you are!"

As he spoke Case arose and opened the door. Instantly there tumbled into the cabin a boy of twelve or fourteen — a slender, thin-faced lad whose whole appearance indicated little food and little parental care. He did not rise to his feet.

"Well, what is it?" asked Clay, taking the intruder by the arm. "Why don't you get up and introduce yourself? What do you want here, anyway?"

"Don't switch on the light!" the boy pleaded, as Clay stretched his hand toward the electric switch. "They are watching the boat from the pier, and I don't want them to know I got in. That's why I didn't stand up when the door was opened. The railing of the deck protected me from the view of any one up there. I'm running away!"

"You look the part!" Clay observed, motioning the visitor to a chair. "Why?"

"Because they'll make me tell who stole the diamonds and furs up at Rock Island," was the hesitating reply. "They'll put me in jail if I don't tell!"

"If you know and won't tell," Clay observed, "they surely will put you in jail!"

"Why won't you tell?" asked Alex. "Perhaps you helped do the job yourself!"

"No I didn't!" the boy said.

He was about to say more when there came another voice from outside—a slow, steady voice demanding attention.

"Listen, you kids in there," the voice said. "Listen, and I'll tell you what to do to save a couple of lives!"

CHAPTER II – ALEX. GOES FISHING

"Things seem to be coming our way!" Alex. observed. "Can either of you boys see the fellow who is doing the talking?"

Clay stepped to the cabin door and opened it. The night had fallen swiftly, and the deck was quite dark. The boy started toward the switch which controlled the prow light, but the voice checked him, coming, not from the pier, but from the water at the side of the motor boat.

"Don't turn on any lights!" the voice said. "I'm right here under the overhang. I came to ask you to do me a favor! You look like decent sort of chaps!"

"Thanks for the compliment!" Alex. put in, from the cabin door, where he stood with a freckled nose wrinkled to its full capacity – and then a little more!

"Keep still a minute, can't you?" demanded Clay. "Let us see what it is the man wants us to do for him. Why don't you come on deck?" the boy added, bending over in the hope of getting a view of the strange visitor.

"I don't come on deck," was the reply, "because I'm not lookin' for trouble! I'm in bad here, strangers, an' I want you to take the boy down the river with you!"

The lad who had recently come on board now came up to the cabin door and stood in a listening attitude. In the deep dusk his face could not be seen plainly, but Alex., who stood close to his side, knew that he was shaking with the chill of the water.

"The boy says he is running away," objected Clay, bending still lower over the deck railing. "We are not going to aid in any such a game," he added.

"Shucks!" came the answer, still from the water. "He ain't got nobody nor nothin' to run away from, that kid ain't! Hide him until you get out of Cairo, an' then I may be able to do something for him."

"What's the answer?" Alex. cut in. "Why should he want to be hidden? Perhaps you're the man that robbed the warehouse at Rock Island! He

8

just told us that he knew who did it! Come on deck, and we'll talk it over."

"If you want to get away from Cairo without sampling all the jails in the county," the unseen man continued, "you'll slip anchor an' get down the river right soon! The men who are watchin' you are comin' down the pier now. I reckon they saw me talking from the bosom of the river. Before I duck under an' head for Missouri, I'll tell you that the kid you've got there is O. K. Take him along with you!"

Then, much to the amazement of the boys on the motor boat, a shot came out of the darkness in the direction of the pier, and a bullet cut the water close to where the man lay, near the prow, half afloat and half clinging to the hull of the Rambler.

"You see!" the unseen man said. "Drop down until this excitement is over!"

"That's a cheerful kind of a merman," Alex. declared. "He heard the shot and took his own advice to disappear, anyway! What do you think of him? Heading a lot of gunmen in this direction an' then advising us to run away!"

For a moment nothing was heard save the sighing of the wind and the wash of the river. Lights were showing in the city, which was not far from the pier, and one large street lamp disclosed the figures of a dozen men running toward the motor boat! The man who had done the shooting stood near the foot of the pier, a revolver in his hand. Clay sprang for the switch which controlled the prow light.

"That's more like it!" came a voice from the shore, as the light flared out on the cluttered pier and the swirling waters of the river. "Why didn't you do that before?"

"Quit your shooting and come on board!" Clay advised. "We understand the use of firearms ourselves! Come aboard and tell us what all this is about."

"We'll come, fast enough!" said one of the advancing party. "Keep your lights on."

In a minute more the little motor boat was crowded with rough-looking men, all armed, and all insisting that every nook and corner of the Rambler should be searched.

The boys offered no objections, but sat on the deck railing waiting for the men to perform their task and go away. Captain Joe and Teddy, however, objected strenuously, and it required the efforts of all four, before the search was completed, to keep the pets from being shot by those whose legs had been nipped by sharp teeth.

Finally one of the men, who seemed to be in command, demanded of Clay:

"Where did the boy who came on board go?"

"He must have gone into the river," was the reply. "Just after the shooting I looked for him, but he was not here. Who is he, and what is he wanted for?"

"He belongs to the man who robbed the warehouse office up at Rock Island," was the gruff reply. "If you shelter him you'll be breaking the law. What was that swimmer saying to you?" the fellow continued. "That's the man we want! Why should he come to you, anyway?"

"I don't know why he should come to us any more than I know why you men should come on board with your insulting suspicions," Clay answered. "When you make up your minds that neither the man nor the boy is here, we'll go on down the river."

The search continued for some moments, and the men reluctantly went ashore.

"Honest!" Alex. then asked of Clay. "Honest, now! Where did the boy go?"

"He must have taken a jump into the river," was the boy's reply. "He certainly is not on board the Rambler. He just disappeared when those men appeared."

"Then he's probably drowned!" Alex. commented. "No one could swim long in that current. And the man, too, probably went under! Too bad!" he added, soberly.

"Well," Clay declared, "I've got enough of the hospitality of this city. Suppose we drop down to-night? It will be risky sailing because of the flood, but at the same time it may keep us all out of jail. Those men may come back after they get a few more drinks."

The Rambler was a staunch little motor boat, fully competent to make her way in almost any body of water, but the boys were afraid of driftwood and wreckage, and also of running off into bayous which ran out into swamps for miles, with almost as strong a current as the main channel. Those who have read previous volumes of this series will doubtless recall the adventures of the four boys in Brazil on the Amazon river, on the Columbia river, far up in British Columbia, and on the Colorado river, as far up as the Grand Canyon.

A month before that night in Cairo, the boys had launched the motor boat on the Mississippi far up near its source. They had struggled with sandbars and falls, but had at last worked round the Falls of St. Anthony and struck better water. They had met with plenty of adventures on the way, but nothing of the character of the happenings of that evening. The portion of their journey really worthy of record begins at Cairo on this early November night.

The pets, of which the boys were very fond, had, as already stated by one of the boys, been acquired in Brazil and British Columbia, Captain Joe having been bought by Alex. at Para, and Teddy having been rescued from a tree wreck in the great river of the north. Both animals had been taught all sorts of tricks by the boys.

"That's all right, about our being in danger here," Case observed, "but, at the same time, if we leave now, in the night, with the river up, we shall only confirm the suspicions of those on shore. Suppose we move away from this pier, so as to be out of the way of the mob, and anchor in another place, where those whose duty it is to look up suspicious river boats can find us if they desire to? For one, I don't like the idea of being chased down the river."

11

"Solomon had nothing on you!" Alex. agreed. "We may as well remain here until morning. I must confess that I don't like the way the Father of Waters is acting!"

"Well, let us get somewhere and settle down for the night!" Jule suggested. "I'm still hungry! Those fellows spoiled my supper. Who wants more ham?"

"Say," Alex. cried, with one of his inimitable grins, "why not have a fish for supper? I won't be able to sleep much, on account of watching, and may as well have a good square meal! Then I'll sit up and you boys can go to bed."

"Where can you get a fish to-night?" demanded Jule. "Think one is going to climb up on the deck? Ham is good enough for me right now!"

But Alex. did not abandon the idea of having a fish supper. After the Rambler had been taken a short distance up the river and anchored in a little bay which promised protection from the rushing current, loaded at times with driftwood and the wreck of houses and barns, the lad again broached the subject.

"I can get the rowboat out," he insisted, "and let her down stream with a line. Then I can fish under that bank to the east. Don't you ever think all the river fish have moved into top flats because of the flood! I saw one jump up just a moment ago! You boys keep a good fire and I'll guarantee to bring the fish!"

"Go it!" Clay laughed. "I wouldn't go out in a rowboat for a dozen fish suppers, but you seem to have the luck of the Irish on such occasions, so get to going!"

"You'll eat the fish, all right!" Alex. taunted, "so help me get the boat down."

The skiff was lowered from the roof of the little cabin and placed in the water, with a great splash. It tugged and strained at the cord which held it, and now and then received severe bumps from floating debris, but Alex. insisted on drawing it up and jumping in. Then he set about getting his fish for supper!

For a long time the boy fished without receiving any intimation that there was a fish left in the river! The boat caught plenty of driftwood, however. At times great masses of trees and timbers would go sailing down, advancing out of the darkness into the circle of light about the Rambler as if brought to life by the presence of mankind. Then the darkness would receive them again and the water would run clear for a time.

The little bay where the Rambler was moored was in a measure out of the sweep of the strong current, still the water eddied and swirled around the little rowboat in a threatening manner. Sometimes the boy had all he could do to keep the craft from turning turtle and dumping him into the river. The other boys, watching from the deck of the motor boat, often called to him to draw up on the line in order to avoid a mass of wreckage drifting that way.

The strong, high prow-light of the motor boat cast a sharp illumination over the river for some distance up stream, revealing the approach of dangerous wreckage, and the lone fisherman was often glad to heed the warnings of his chums. At last, however, just as he was playing a fish which seemed to him as large as a whale, and twice as ferocious, he heard a call which he disregarded for a second.

"There's a roof coming down!" Clay shouted to the boy. "It is likely to pay you a visit! Better come aboard!"

"And there's something moving on it!" Jule shouted. "It looks like a baby!"

Alex. was busy with his line. The fish supper was almost in sight! If he heard what was said to him he did not heed the warning, for he kept on playing his fish, which seemed inclined to take the rowboat down the river to the Gulf of Mexico!

The piece of roof to which the boys pointed swung around the side of the Rambler and was pulled in toward the shore by the eddy which had drawn so many lesser objects in. Then, for the first time, Alex. saw his danger. If the mass struck the boat it might crush it. At the very least it would be likely to break the line with which it was attached to the Rambler and send him adrift!

The boy seized the cable and began to draw the boat up to the Rambler, seeking protection under its bulk. Then he heard a cry come from the raft, and saw a mite of a boy reaching out his hands. The boat dropped back and the mass, edging in below the Rambler, struck it full on the prow!

CHAPTER III — A WAIF FROM THE RIVER

The cable tying the rowboat to the Rambler parted with a snap as the wreckage struck the light craft, and Alex. went rocking and bobbing down toward the Gulf of Mexico! The boys on the Rambler saw him get out an oar to secure steerway, though he was pressed on by the house roof which had done the mischief.

It was not a flat roof, but one with two steep sides and a sharp apex. It rode the current apex up, as if floating on a floor crossing under the eaves. On the top of the ridge-boards, clinging on with hands and bare heels, and shouting fit to wake the people of Cairo, the lads on the Rambler saw a half-dressed negro boy of perhaps ten or eleven years. The more the roof bobbed on the waves the louder he yelled.

When the line snapped Clay rushed to the motors and turned on full power. The Rambler trembled as she thrust her nose against the current, wavered, and then, answering her helm, swung around broadside to the sweep of water, shook a mass of wreckage from her prow, as a dog shakes off water, and edged down stream.

In a minute after the accident the powerful motor boat was chasing Alex., the little negro boy, and the teetering roof down toward Memphis! It was dark on the river, and the roaring of the waters made the prospect doubly disagreeable. The current was running fast, and that one minute of getting under way had swept the rowboat some distance down stream. Still it was just visible under the strong prow light.

"There's Alex.'s fish!" shouted Chase, pointing to the cowering negro boy on the apex of the roof. "Wonder how he wants him cooked for supper?"

"The last find Alex. made," Jule laughed, "was a bear! What will he be finding next? S-a-a-y, you coon!" he called out, shaping his hands for a trumpet in order to direct his voice, "don't you go to dropping off! We'll pick you up with the motor boat," he continued, as the little fellow began scrambling toward the water's edge.

15

"There he goes!" shouted Clay, as the negro boy, not heeding Jule's directions, went clattering down the shingles and dropped into the river. "The little fellow was afraid we would go away and leave him! What do you think of that?" he added. "The coon is swimming like a fish to the rowboat!"

The boy would have reached the rowboat handily if a heavy piece of timber had not intervened. It struck him head-on as he swam, and he went under the brown waters. Then the boys on the Rambler saw Alex. throw off his coat, take the broken line between his teeth, and dive into the river, just missing the great timber as he went headfirst into the flood! There was a growl and a snarl on deck, and then Captain Joe and Teddy Bear were both in the river, swimming down toward the swaying roof.

The bulldog, with the instinct of the intelligent canine, doubtless recognized the peril of the situation and took to the water on an errand of rescue, but with the bear it was different. He had been patiently taught to bathe and play in the water with the boys, and now he saw only a frolic ahead!

However this may be, it was the bear cub who seized the negro boy as he came to the surface, half supported by Alex.'s arm. The little fellow had not been rendered unconscious by the blow he had received, and was able to sustain himself in the water as soon as he came to the surface.

Alex. was busy hauling the boat back, or trying to, with the end of the line in one hand, and Captain Joe swam directly to him. He knew that if he released the line the rowboat would drift away, leaving him and his companions to be rescued by the Rambler, and he had a stubborn notion that he would like to get out of the mess without the assistance of his chums! They would then have no opportunity to make sly remarks about his skill as a fisherman! The fishline was wound around his left arm, and he believed that the fish he had been playing when the accident took place was still on the hook!

The situation was clearing, for Alex. held to the line, and boy, bear, dog, and frightened negro boy, were doing very well in the swift current when another mass of wreckage came sweeping down upon them. As it came down Alex. dove under, and the negro boy started to do the same, but just then his eyes fell on the bear, hanging to his arm, and with a scream which only half disclosed how scared he was he scrambled on the floating heap of brush and was swept down stream!

His round eyes were, apparently, as large as saucers and as white as chalk as he turned to see Teddy Bear pursuing him to his place of refuge. Familiar with the water game, the bear chased the negro boy to the limit of the wreckage and pushed him in with his nose. By this time Alex. was clinging to the rowboat, with Captain Joe serving as chaperon, and theRambler was at hand, the boys on board cheering Teddy and the negro boy as they chased around the brush heap from which they had been pitched into the river. Although they called out to the boy not to be afraid of the bear, his cries rose above the roar of the waters!

Alex. and Captain Joe were picked up first, the rowboat made secure, and then the Rambler rounded the floating mass of brush and took Teddy on board. The little fellow scrambled away from the hands reached out to grasp him, his eyes following the figure of the bear as it was lifted on deck.

"Fo' de Lawd's sake!" he gasped, his eyes round and white, "don' yo' feed dis coon to dat bear! He sure done eat dis chile!"

When passed up to the deck the boy gave one look at the bear, let out another yell of fright, and, ducking into the cabin, dodged under the table, where he crouched on hands and knees, his eyes sticking out like white doorknobs. The boys were too full of laugh for the time being to try to explain matters to him.

As soon as Alex. was on deck he began unwinding the fishline from his arm. Then he played it over the side of the boat, much to the amusement of his chums.

"Perhaps you think I didn't catch a fish?" the lad demanded, with a wink at Clay.

"If you didn't get a fish," laughed Clay, "it is about the only thing you didn't bring out of the river with you! We fished out a bear, a dog, and a baby coon with you! You surely ought to have a fish!"

And Alex. did have a fish! It was firmly hooked, and came flopping out of the water when he drew in the line. Still under the table, with his eyes on the bear, the rescued negro boy licked his chops when he saw it. Clay observed the action and went to him. After a time the little fellow was coaxed out of his hiding-place.

"That's a pet bear!" explained Clay. "He won't bite you!"

The boy seemed to want to believe the other, for the sake of the fish supper which appeared to be coming soon, but he edged away from the cub, all the same!

"You hungry?" asked Case, coming up.

The little fellow nodded, and Case went on.

"What's your name?"

"Abraham Lincoln Charles Sumner Horace Greeley Banks!"

The little chap repeated the names in a sing-song tone, with the air of one who had been carefully drilled in the repetition. The boys broke into shouts of laughter, and even Teddy Bear nosed his way through the little group and stood gazing at the negro boy with reproving eyes! The boy tried to dodge away, but Clay held him fast.

"Jerusalem!" Case cried, as soon as he could control his voice. "What a name! Where did you get it, chile?"

"Mah mammy done 'stowed it on me!" was the reply.

"Well, it is too long," Clay decided, "so we'll just call you Mose! Do you happen to be hungry, little one?" he added, with a glance at the fish.

In answer the boy laid his hands on the region of his stomach and grinned.

"Where do you live?" asked Alex., ringing the water out of his clothes, which had been removed as soon as he reached the deck. "What will your mammy say to your going off on the river? She'll wallop you, chile, good an' plenty!"

"I done run away!" answered the boy.

"That's two to-night!" grinned Alex., preparing to dress the fish for supper. "How many more are we likely to find before we get to the Gulf?"

Teddy Bear, who seemed to feel that he was deserving of some attention for having rescued Mose from instant death in the river, now came up and brushed his soft nose over the boys' hand. Mose's eyes grew wider, but, seeing that the bear did not offer to bite, he ventured to stroke his head, whereat the cub sat up on his hind feet and asked to have a boxing lesson!

"That bear is a spoiled child!" Case remarked, as Teddy began sparing. "He is no good at all — just a clown!"

"Where did you run from?" asked Jule, anxious to know more of the negro boy.

"San Louee," was the reply. "I done lived on th' levee!"

"From St. Louis, eh?" Clay said. "Where do you want to go?"

"I done hire out to you all," was the reply.

"Of course!" Alex. laughed. "Didn't we bring him up out of the waters? He'll make a fine playmate for Teddy Bear!"

"If he doesn't disappear, as that other waif did," smiled Clay.

"Where do you suppose that boy went to?" asked Alex. "He never swam to shore, that is, to the other shore, and if he had landed on the pier when the men came on board they would certainly have seen him. I reckon the darkness just ate him!"

"And the man who came to speak a good word for him!" Clay went on. "If he had been the thief wanted for the Rock Island diamond and fur robbery, he couldn't have been more mysterious. The boy said he would be made to tell about the robbery if they found him, and this man wanted to get him out of the way, so I guess we can put the pieces

19

together and patch out the truth. The man is one of the robbers and the boy belongs to him!"

"If I had the Sherlock genius you toss out so easily," Jule cut in, "I'd put it in a book. Why should the robber come to us to speak a good word for the boy? He ought to have known that we'd see through the game."

"He may not be the robber at all," Case observed. "There was some mystery connected with the two, and that's all we know about it! The man is gone, and the boy is gone, and they are probably drowned, so we may as well count the story closed."

"I'll go you a dinner at the Bismark, as soon as we get back to Chicago," Clay insisted, "that we find both the man and the boy before we get down to the Gulf!"

"You're in for the dinners, then!" Case exclaimed. "And now," he went on, "what are we going to do to-night? Are we going on down the river, or are we going to get into some cozy little slip and anchor for the second time?"

"I'm no good Solomon on an empty stomach," laughed Clay. "Wait until Alex. has his fish supper served! You want some, too, don't you Mose?" he added, turning to the little fellow, who stood gazing from the bear to the fish, now ready for the pan.

"I's done gone empty cl'ar to mah toes!" was Mose's reply.

After the fish had been eaten Mose was put to bed in one of the bunks, and the boys decided to go on down the river. They wanted to get away from any such entanglement as had been suggested by the visit of the officers and the search of the motor boat.

They made a long distance with little trouble, as they were going with the driftwood, and at daylight tied up in a small bayou, at the end of which a deserted old house stood lowering down upon the flood with a touch of mystery in the broken windows and overhanging eaves!

CHAPTER IV – TWO BOYS GET A TUMBLE

"I'd give a cent to know just where we are!" Jule declared, as he stood on the deck of the Rambler, waiting for Case's call to breakfast, the advance odors of which were creeping out of the cabin, where Mose and Teddy Bear lay on a rug together, evidently the very best of friends!

"Give me the coin, then," Alex. exclaimed. "We are about ten or fifteen miles below Hickman, Kentucky, and we are on the Missouri side; and there's a loop of river which runs north a long way and comes back again. Some day the Mississippi will cut through the neck of land, and then there'll be another large island, with houses set back from the river a long distance! Give me the cent!"

Jule gravely passed the coin over to Alex., who as gravely pocketed it, and drew Jule to a seat beside himself on the gunwale of the boat. Captain Joe came up to the boys as they sat there and wagged his tail, his nose pointing toward the deserted old house at the end of the bayou.

"Do you see what the bulldog wants?" Alex. asked, in a moment.

"He wants a run on shore," replied Jule. "He wants to get off the boat and do stunts on the grass. I'm with him in that, too!"

"He's pointing to the old house!" Alex. suggested, with a grin.

"Good idea!" winked Jule. "Suppose we go over to the ranch and see what sort of a place it is? We'll just sneak off after breakfast and be back in an hour."

"Right," agreed Alex. "We may find a buried treasure! Or plunder from the Rock Island warehouse may be hidden in some dusty attic! What? That sounds like a story of John Paul Jones, out of a book!"

"I reckon all we'll find will be rats," the practical Jule replied. "But I like to ramble over old houses. It evidently used to stand on the bank of the river, but some washout left it back so far that it was deserted. It looks like there might be ghosts hiding in it right now! Do you hear anything?" the boy added, as he bent his ear toward the neglected mansion, sinking to decay now for many a long year. "Do you hear anything that sounds uncanny? I thought I heard a ghost call!"

"I half believe you mean it!" laughed Alex. "I believe you really think you hear something ghostly! If I were rich once for every ghost there is in the world, I wouldn't have a cent to my name! What does this ghost call sound like?" added the boy.

"It sounded like a long, low call for help!" was the reply. "I believe all the calls from deserted houses are long and low, what?"

"Right you are!" Alex. answered. "Say, what's the matter of taking Captain Joe with us when we go to the house? If there's a ghost behind the casings, he'll be certain to find and bring it out to us!"

"Then I'm strong for Captain Joe!" cried Jule. "We'll bring the perturbed spirit on board and put it with our collection of animals! And there's the breakfast call, at last!" he continued, whereat both boys rushed into the cabin.

Clay, who had been tinkering around the motors for half an hour, entered the cabin before breakfast was over, his face looking troubled, his clothing smeared with grease.

"I have an idea that we'll stop here a few days until some one goes to one of the towns hereabouts and brings back some bolts," he said. "The motors are out of whack, and ought not to be operated in the shape they are in."

"I'll go back to Hickman in the rowboat," declared Case. "I have a notion that I'd like to see the town."

"And row against that current?" asked Alex. "I see you doing it!"

"You couldn't do it in a thousand years!" Jule observed.

"Well," Case went on, looking at his map of the river, "there's New Madrid, on the Missouri side. I might walk up there and back in a day."

"Up there?" laughed Alex., looking over Case's shoulder. "Why do you say up there? New Madrid is north from here, all right, but it is down stream, for all that!"

"Well, walk down there, then!" Case replied. "I want to learn something about that robbery anyway, and there may be news of it; besides, a walk along the river will be a sort of a picnic. It isn't more than ten or twelve miles to the town."

"Then you'd better arrange to return to-morrow," Clay advised. "You are not used to such long walks. We are in no hurry to go on, for we have all the time there is until this time next year!"

So it was finally arranged that Case should walk down to New Madrid and get the needed repairs for the motors, while the others looked over the country which lay about them. When Alex. suggested the visit to the deserted house, Clay was anxious to become one of the party. He said he had had the same idea in his mind ever since seeing the old place.

"After Case goes," Jule suggested, "that would leave only Mose and Teddy Bear on board the Rambler. I don't believe it is safe to leave her alone."

"Of course it isn't," Clay admitted, "so I'll remain here to-day and visit the old building to-morrow. Then you two boys can remain at home."

Everything being satisfactorily arranged, Alex. and Jule started away up the bayou in the rowboat. The old basin was full of water, and so there was little current, which made it easy rowing. In half an hour they were at the foot of an old pier, slanting over on weak legs like a tipsy man. It was plain that the landing had not been used for commercial purposes for a long time.

The boys fastened the boat and ran briskly up the rotting footway which led to the enclosure in which the old house stood. There was a wilderness of trees and shrubs in the enclosure, and the walks, which had evidently once been carefully tended, were now overgrown with weeds and long grass. Lizards darted out of unseen places and sped away as the boys advanced along a broken walk which led to the front door of the mansion.

At the very threshold the boys paused, listening. The ragged blinds were flapping in the breeze, and the trees which rimmed the enclosure rustled and creaked in a most uncanny way, but these sounds were not the ones which brought the adventurous boys to a halt.

The noise they heard sounded like the tones of a violin, coming from a great distance. The notes, faint, sweet, perplexing, rose and fell on the wind, now lifting into a weird song, now dropping to the softest melody!

"There's some one here, after all!" Jule suggested, though there was a question in the way the words were spoken. "Some one lives here? What do you think?"

Alex. pointed to the broken door which opened into the disordered hall, to the window blinds, beating the casings at the will of the wind, and at the long grass and weeds growing between the planks and stones of the walks.

"I don't believe any one lives here!" he insisted.

"Then what is it making the music?" demanded Jule. "If that isn't some one playing the violin you may eat my head for a cabbage!"

They listened again. The sounds stopped directly, then there came a banging of doors and a rustle, as if some one in trailing clothes was being dragged through the hall. Then a shriek which appeared to come from directly under the feet of the boys cut the air, lifting into a terrifying yell at the end. The lads involuntarily started back down the path, but both stopped and faced the house again.

"I'm not going away without knowing more about it!" Alex. declared.

"That's the way I look at it!" grinned Jule. "We can't turn tail and run like a couple of cowards. I wish we had brought Captain Joe along with us!"

"Clay wanted him for company," Alex. explained. "Joe looked like his heart was broken when we came off without him! I'll bet he runs away and comes after us!"

Seeing that their automatic revolvers were in working order, the boys walked back up the broken walk, mounted the steps, and passed into the ancient hallway of the mansion. All was ruin and decay there. The floor was broken out in places, and there were marks of an axe on the casings of the door and on the narrow windows beside it.

The stairway leading to the rooms above was broken, too, some of the steps being gone entirely. The lads stopped at the foot of the steps for an instant to gaze upward and then turned into a lofty room on the left. This must have been the parlor, and the apartment beyond it must have been the library.

The furniture, which had once been valuable, was broken into bits, and a charred spot on the floor showed where a fire had been kindled. The rooms on that floor were all desolate and dismantled, and the boys soon turned their attention to those above the ruined staircase.

Scarcely had they gained the head of the stairs when the music began again. It seemed to come down the wide hallway which ran nearly through the house parallel with the front.

"We're getting nearer to the band!" Jule whispered.

There was such a hush over the place, such a weird, uncanny atmosphere, that, somehow, the boys did not feel like being loud-voiced or boisterous.

"We'll be running into a reception committee next!" Alex. returned.

The music continued for a few seconds, then ended in a repetition of the dragging, rustling sound and the shriek which had been heard before. This time the noise indicating physical motion appeared to come from the very hallway where the boys were standing!

Alex. and Jule continued on through the hall until they came to a partition which shut off the north end of it. There was a door in this partition, but it was locked. At first all the efforts of the lads failed to budge it.

"There's one part of the ranch that hasn't rotted away," Alex. observed, as red-faced and perspiring, he paused in his attack on the door.

"That shows there's some one taking care of it," Jule decided. "Suppose we try the door once more? It ought to give way before our weight."

They both threw their shoulders against the upper panels and they dropped back, revealing a small room which had the appearance of having recently been occupied. There was a wide fireplace at the back of the room, which was at the end of the house, and a chair standing near the hearth was softly cushioned. There was a window on each side of the fireplace, but the curtains were drawn so all the details of the apartment were not visible. The boys drew back for an instant.

"We're breaking into some one's house!" Jule whispered.

"I guess that's right!" Alex. returned. "What ought we to do now?"

"Keep right on until we get at the solution of the mystery," Jule answered. "It may be that we shall find a maiden in distress, and — —"

The boy stopped in the midst of his light-hearted speech and looked again through the broken panels of the door at the end of the hall. What he saw was a side door opening.

As the door swung back an old man, white haired and walking with a stout cane, came into the room and sat down in the chair by the hearth. Then, without glancing toward the broken panels and the boys beyond, he spoke:

"The door is not fastened, boys. You are welcome to enter."

The boys entered, feeling ashamed and half afraid, and the old man pointed to two chairs by the hearth which had not been seen through the broken door.

"Sit down!" he said, almost with an air of command, "and tell me why you are here."

The boys sank down into the chairs; then there came a sharp click, and they felt themselves falling through the floor!

CHAPTER V – A NEW CAPTAIN ON BOARD

Clay continued his work on the motors for a long time after the departure of Alex. and Jule. It was impossible to make them work with safety without the repairs Case had gone after, but the boy decided that the present would be a fine time to clean them.

While he worked, polishing and oiling, Mose and Teddy came out of the cabin arm-in-arm! At least the little negro boy had one arm around the cub's neck!

"You've got over your scare, eh?" Clay laughed, as the two came to his side.

"Ah sure tu'n white las' night!" Mose declared, rolling his eyes until they looked like white billiard balls. "Ah's so scared!"

"You are black enough this morning," Clay suggested. "Where did you come from?"

"Ah done come f'm San Louee," was the reply. "Ah lib on de levee."

"Did you run away from St. Louis?" asked Clay. "Did you come all the way from the levee on the roof Alex. fished you off from?"

Mose, still playing with the cub, explained that he had sneaked on board a steamer at St. Louis, but had been put ashore at a landing above Cairo by the mate. Then, so great had been his desire to get farther south for the winter, he had taken a drifting boat and pushed out into the swollen stream.

The boat had been crushed in a mass of wreckage, but the boy had managed to crawl up on the floating roof where he had been found. The mammy he had spoken of as having been so liberal with him in the bestowal of names was an old colored lady who had given him a place to sleep on cold nights and occasionally fed him when he was hungry. He knew nothing of his parents or any relatives. He was just a levee waif.

After a time Clay went to the cabin and lay on his bunk, which let down from the ceiling, being usually drawn up during the daytime. The motors were still under process of cleaning, and various parts lay scattered about.

Presently the boy heard a great racket on deck. Captain Joe's deep voice came in threatening growls, and Mose and Teddy scampered into the cabin. Clay sprang to his feet and made for the deck, not doubting that Alex. and Jule had returned and were up to some mischief. Before he reached the door he heard the sound of a heavy blow.

He could see no one through the doorway, which Mose had left open, although most of the deck was in sight, yet the blow he had heard warned him that something out of the ordinary was taking place. He stepped back to a shelf for his revolver.

He knew that during floods bands of outlaws frequented the river in quest of plunder, and it was his first impression that one of these had discovered the motor boat and was trying to board her. He wondered at the silence of the dog.

As the boy reached for his weapon, a gruff voice from the cabin doorway commanded him to face about and hold up his hands.

"And hold 'em up empty, too!" the gruff voice said.

There was nothing for Clay to do but to obey. It was with an effort, however, that he kept his arms extended. The leering eyes of the man with the face of a fox who stood before him with a revolver pushed almost into his face caused such hot surges of rage to fill the boy's brain that he came near facing the peril and springing upon the outlaw.

Mose, levee bred and wise to the unlawful purpose of the intruder, moved stealthily toward the shelf where Clay's revolver lay, in plain sight. In another second it would have been in the little fellow's hand, with what result Clay could not imagine, but the outlaw saw the movement and edged forward, still keeping the revolver leveled at Clay, much to the latter's disgust.

"Here, you coon!" the man shouted, "get over in that corner and stay there! Move, or I'll give you a lift!"

The brute gave Mose a savage kick in the side as he spoke. It was one thing for Clay to be placed in a humiliating position, to be threatened with a gun, but it was quite another for him to stand inactive and see a boy brutally treated! Disregarding all his thoughts of the uselessness of the move, the boy sprang at the outlaw.

Although only a boy, Clay was muscular and in training. The man he had attacked was stronger and heavier than the lad, but he was slower of movement, and the result of the conflict might have been a victory for Clay if the two had been permitted to continue the struggle unmolested.

While the meager furniture of the little cabin was being broken and tossed hither and yon by the combatants, while Teddy was jumping about, eager to get hold of one of the fighters—as he had been taught to do when the boys were wrestling—and while Mose was doing his best to get over to the shelf where the revolver lay, there came a quick jar on deck, a jar caused by the bunting of a boat against the hull of the Rambler, and then hurrying footsteps on the forward deck.

Clay fought all the harder when the sounds reached his ears, for he was sure that Alex. and Jule had returned, and that short work would now be made of the intruder. He was gradually securing a hold on his enemy which would have ended the battle when he was seized and lifted—by a giant, it seemed to him—clear of the cabin deck and held there while the outlaw slowly regained his feet and picked up his weapon.

Clay saw that it was the other side that had received the reinforcements, and motioned to Mose to remain quiet and keep out of sight. He feared that further activity on the part of the negro boy would add to his punishment.

After catching his breath, the outlaw with whom Clay had been struggling lifted a pair of bloodshot eyes to Clay's face and sprang at him, his huge fists clenched until the knuckles showed hard and white.

"You bum!" he shouted, lunging at the lad, "I'll give you some of your own medicine! What do you mean by striking me?"

The blow would have landed squarely in the boy's face, but the man who had picked him off the outlaw warded it off with a fist like a ham, and set the boy behind the great bulk of his own person. Clay was encouraged by this defense, and began hoping that he had found a friend instead of another enemy.

But this hope was soon shattered, for the newcomer produced a hard cord, which had evidently once been used as a fishline, and coolly proceeded to tie the boy's wrists. This task completed to his satisfaction, he pushed the boy over on his bunk and tossed Mose on top of him.

"There!" he cried. "You keep quiet, or I'll turn Sam loose on you! And, Sam, if you molest the boy again I'll settle with you for it. I take it he had a right to fight for his boat! And the little coon! You keep your hands off him, too!"

The man called Sam flashed an ugly look out of his foxy, inflamed eyes and went out on deck. In a moment he was seen in the doorway again, dragging Captain Joe after him.

"Shall I pitch the dog overboard?" he asked, in a surly tone. "He took a piece out of my leg and I gave him a rap on the head. He's knocked out!"

Clay sat up on the bunk and glared at the man, who was still holding the bulldog by the collar. At that moment, whatever the consequences, the fellow's life would not have been worth a farthing if the boy had had a gun!

"Don't let him kill the dog!" Clay said, appealing to the giant. "He's a good fellow, that dog! Of course he bit that robber! He wouldn't have been a good dog if he hadn't. Take what you want on the boat, but let the dog live."

The giant, who was at least six foot six inches in height and large in proportion, looked Captain Joe over after the manner of one acquainted with dogs while Clay awaited his decision anxiously.

"The kid is right," he finally declared. "This is a good dog, and we'll keep him with us. Took a piece out of your leg, did he?"

The big fellow placed his hands on his mammoth hips, threw back his head until his hairy throat rose like a sturdy column of strength, and poured forth such a torrent of laughter that Teddy came out of the cabin to see what new sport was being prepared for his amusement. Sam struck at the cub, but the other pushed him away before he had done any mischief.

"That's a good one!" roared the giant. "Took a piece out of your leg, did he? If he ain't pizened, and lives after that, I'll keep him. There's a heap of pizen snakes down my way that need looking after. Took a piece out of your leg! That's too good for anything! Ho! Ho! Ho! Took a piece out of your leg!"

"I hope he'll some day take a piece out of that throat of yours!" roared Sam.

"No doubt, no doubt!" replied the giant. "He may be a doin' of it when the hangman is busy puttin' a new hemp tie about that weazen of yours! Now let the kids and the dog and bear alone, and help work the boat out into the current. We've got to be getting out of this!"

"You'll have to put the motors together before you move her," Sam replied.

The giant looked thoughtfully at the scattered fragments, then at Clay, still in the bunk, and scratched a thatch of red hair which looked like a hayrick.

"It seems to need puttin' together," he said, beckoning to Clay.

Then the boy saw that it was the intention of the outlaws to take possession of the Rambler and shift her down stream before any of the boys returned. He thought of Alex. and Jule, marooned on that desolate point of land where the old house stood, of Case, trudging back from New Madrid with the repairs to find the boat gone!

He glanced about hopelessly, searching the shores of the bayou on the faint chance of seeing Alex. and Jule returning. Captain Joe was now regaining consciousness in the cabin, and Teddy was trying to interest him in a boxing match! Mose sat in a corner motionless, except that his eyes rolled about in anger or panic, the boy could not determine which.

"Well, get the engines together!" ordered the giant.

"There are parts missing," Clay answered. "One of the boys has gone to New Madrid for repairs. She won't run a foot without them."

Sam and the giant conversed together for a moment, and then the former called out to Mose, emphasizing his words with a threatening gesture:

"Here, coon!" he shouted. "Can you swim?"

"Ah sho' can," was the reply.

"Then jump ashore and take this dog with you. If I ever see either of you again I'll take your hides off!"

"It would improve matters to hold 'em under a while!" he added, angrily.

"I won't have it," the giant returned. "No murder for me!"

"You'll see what'll come of lettin' 'em go!" Sam warned.

"Git!" ordered the big fellow, in a not unkind tone, and Mose, nothing loth, gathered the dog in his arms and leaped into the bayou.

Clay almost held his breath for a moment, until he saw that the cold water had revived the dog, and that he was swimming. Then his attention was attracted to the outlaws, who were, with pole and oar, edging the Rambler out into the river.

He believed that the boat would be wrecked the moment it, helpless, struck the mass of floodwood sweeping down. Presently he felt the push of the current, and the boat went whirling down stream, tipping from side to side as she spun around, helpless in the current.

Then a great tree struck the stern and half capsized her. The end seemed at hand.

CHAPTER VI – CAPTAIN JOE MAKES A HIT

While the Rambler, in charge of reckless river pirates, was swinging down with the current, threatening to capsize every instant, Alex. and Jule sat flat on a rotten, yielding floor somewhere in the interior of the deserted house, feeling tenderly over their limbs to see if they had received severe injuries during the fall from the room where they had been so inhospitably welcomed by the aged man.

The boys had not fallen far. In fact, it seemed to them that they had only slid down a gentle incline to the story below. A hatch in the floor in front of the hearth had been dropped back, and their chairs had slid into a chute which seemed, from its smoothness, to be in frequent use.

For a minute the boys were alarmed, excited, angry, then the humor of their sudden removal from the apartment above appealed to them. Alex. was first to speak.

"Vot iss?" he exclaimed. "This must be a page of a comic section in one of the Chicago newspapers. How many legs and arms have you broken?"

"Not a one!" answered Jule. "What kind of hospital treatment do you require?"

"If I felt any better," laughed Alex., "I wouldn't know what to take for it."

It was dark as pitch where the boys were, and they felt about until their hands touched. The personal contact gave them new courage.

"What do you make of it?" asked Jule. "This doesn't look good to me!"

"We've simply butted in on some other fellow's game," Alex. replied. "We seem to have visited a crank who thinks it best to be prepared in advance for unwelcome guests."

"A moonshiner or a river pirate!" Jule suggested.

"That's about it!" Alex. answered. "We've interrupted the industry of a set of illicit whisky makers or warehouse thieves. The valley is said to swarm with bandits whenever the river is out of its banks. Now, the question is how are we going to get out and back to the Rambler?"

They did not know that at that moment Clay and the motor boat were in a situation far more serious than that in which they now found themselves!

"I wish it wasn't so dark here!" Jule whispered.

"Why the soft pedal?" asked Alex. "We've got a right to talk as loudly as we like, I take it, being alone in a dark old donjon keep!"

"There's some one in the room with us!" Jule explained, in a whisper which barely reached his chum's ears, so faint it was. "I hear him breathing."

"Hello!" Alex. called out, then. "Hello! Come on out an' be a good fellow!"

There was no answer, and then Alex., reaching into a capacious pocket, brought out a small electric torch and pushed the button. On board the Rambler or on shore, it was a rule of the boys never to move about without an electric torch and an automatic revolver ready for use.

When the light flashed out, its round circle showed only a room twenty feet square in size, with bare discolored walls. Plastering hung to broken lath, so they knew that they were on the ground floor of the deserted house, and not in the cellar. The floor was worn, and the rough boards which half protected the broken windows showed signs of having been long in position. There was no furniture at all in the place.

"Looks like we might rip off a board and walk out," Jule said, still speaking in a very low tone of voice.

"Don't you ever think we're not watched!" Alex. hastened to say. "I don't know but I made a mistake in showing this light."

"There's only one way to discover whether we are watched or not," said the other, "and that is to try to get away. I'm going after that window."

As Jule spoke he moved toward a window which seemed to open on the bayou, as a gleam of water could be seen through the cracks in the window-guard. The instant his hand touched a crumbling board a voice came out of the darkness.

"I wouldn't do that, boys!"

That was all. Jule stopped at the uncanny interruption with a hand suspended in air, and Alex. quickly flashed his light in the direction from which the sound had come.

There was no one in sight. Rats or other creeping, crawling, things seemed to be working in the disreputable walls, for there was a continuous scratching noise, but there were no other sounds. Alex. shut off the light and sat down on the floor again.

"I guess it is no use!" he said. "We'll have to surrender!"

"There will always be someone here to see that you don't get away!" said the voice. "If you make any trouble, you won't get anything to eat! Now, be good!"

"You can keep me as gentle as a lamb by feeding me right!" Alex. said, with a chuckle which was rather forced. "Why don't you show up?"

"You'll see me soon enough," the voice went on. "In the meantime, don't show that electric light again, and if you have any weapons lay them on the floor in this corner."

"I haven't any," lied Alex. "I brought the light instead."

As he spoke the boy nudged Jule, and he, understanding, slid his revolver along the floor in the direction of the voice. It struck against the wall with a metallic thud.

"That's right!" the voice in the darkness said. "Now, you with the light, send it over here. I might want to use it!"

Alex. slid his torch along the floor. In its progress the button was pressed and a round illumination sprang up on the wall. Almost in the center of this they saw the white hair and beard of the old man who had invited them into the room above!

The boys sat for a long time in serious thought after that, well knowing that every word uttered would be heard by their guardian. Alex. was more than hopeful in his views of the situation.

"If these fellows were professionals," he mused, "they wouldn't take any chances on us not having more weapons and more lights. They would make sure by searching us! I don't believe they ever took a prisoner before, or that they are very anxious about keeping us. I guess we just butted in where we're not wanted, and they'll let us go after a time. Anyway, they're easy!"

Directly loud noises were heard in the old house, and the insecure walls shook under heavy burdens. It seemed to the listening lads that huge boxes and barrels were being transferred from one room to another.

There were excited voices, too, although no words could be understood. It seemed to the two prisoners that the old mansion was being deserted, and their impression was that the thieves were removing their plunder because their hiding-place had been intruded upon. In that case, they thought, they might soon be released.

After what seemed a whole day, food was pushed into the room, and the boys ate heartily of the fresh pork sausages, corn pones, and sweet potatoes given them.

"You're all right on the feed!" Alex. called back in the direction of the corner where for an instant the old man had been seen.

There was no answer, but, somehow, the boys were convinced that there was some one there in the room with them. It does not always require the eyes, or the hands, or the ears, or the sense of smell, to show one that others are close by.

There is a tingling of the nerves which warns of the presence of hostile elements, and this it was which showed the prisoners that they were still under guard.

That was a long afternoon. For the most part there were no sounds in the old house; still, now and then, there came the jar of heavy burdens on the floors, and the sharp and angry voices of men, speaking in a tongue the boys did not understand.

When the cracks in the boards at the windows began to darken, they knew that night was falling. They thought of the comfortable cabin of the Rambler, and of the companionship of the other boys with spasms of anger and regret. As the darkness became more complete outside, they arose and walked up and down the floor of their little room.

"Say, Mister!" Alex. called out to their invisible guard, directly, "how many acts are there in this drama? When do the persecuted c-h-e-i-l-d-s return to their agonized and heart-broken parents?"

"I'm as weary of it as you are!" was the remarkable answer, still in that calm voice they had heard before.

"Then why don't you cut it out?" asked Jule.

"There are men in the party who advise that," was the significant answer. "They are at present discussing your fate. Many declare that it is not wise to permit you to leave the place! I'm sorry for you, but you had no right to snoop in here!"

"Next time," Alex. replied, "you hoist a piracy flag, and we'll keep away."

"When will this strategy board you refer to make a report?" asked Jule.

"I may receive orders at any moment," was the answer.

Silence followed. There were crunchings and chatterings, in the walls where rodents were busy making nests, but no sound of human action. In the long wait the boys heard a low, inquisitive sniff!

Alex. drew Jule's head over to him and whispered in his ear:

"That's Captain Joe, for a dollar and a half!"

"You're on!" Jule responded. "I'll be glad to lose the bet at that, too!"

"I guess I know that inquisitive snort!" Alex. went on. "Besides, I told you that the dog would find some way to get to us!"

"Aw, Clay sent him!" declared Jule. "He never found his way here alone."

"The boys may be with him," Alex. suggested, as the sound came again. "I hope he won't make enough noise to disturb his nibs, over in the corner. Good old dog!"

After a time they heard the patter of the dog's feet, and then the guard whistled softly, as if attempting to make friends with whatever animal was approaching.

"Come here, you foolish dog!" he said. "Why don't you come in out of the dark?"

The pat-pat of the dog's soft feet came nearer, and the guard spoke again:

"How the Old Harry did you get in here?" he demanded. "Whose dog are you, anyway?"

The dog growled and there came a flash of light. The guard, becoming afraid of this thing which had found its way into a room supposed to be secure from intrusion, and had switched on the electric.

The light revealed the two prisoners, grouped together in the middle of the room, the old man, standing with weapon extended and with staring eyes, Captain Joe all ready for a spring, an open window, and, lastly, the black face of Mose overlooking the scene with eyes which seemed too large for his head!

"Get him, Joe!" cried both boys in unison.

The light dropped as the dog leaped, and a revolver clattered to the floor. Alex. had hold of the dog in an instant, his other hand reaching for the rolling flashlight.

"Don't eat him up, Joe!" the boy said, tearing the dog away from the fallen man. Captain Joe fell away with a sullen growl.

"The brute has bitten my arm!" the old man moaned.

"If you remain quiet," Alex. said, "you won't have any more wounds to complain of. We'll just tie you up and get out! After we are gone some one will come and let you out. What sort of a place is this, anyway?"

The old man groaned and made no reply, so the boys secured him and crept out of the window into the darkness.

CHAPTER VII — SEARCHING FOR THE RAMBLER

Case found the walking fairly good and reached New Madrid shortly before noon, having started about 8 o'clock. He procured the supplies for which he had been sent and then sought the hotel and partook of an excellent dinner.

"Now," he thought, "shall I walk back to the Rambler to-night, or shall I remain here and look over the town?"

The question was soon decided, for all there was of the town could be seen in a very short time. At 1 o'clock he started back to the motor boat. At 5 o'clock, just as the sun was setting, he came to the bayou where the Rambler had been anchored.

There was no boat there. The night was falling fast, and the bayou and the river were dimly seen through a slight mist. The boy stood on the bank of the bayou for a long time, studying the situation.

"There's something wrong!" he decided. "The motors could never have been forced into motion with the parts missing! The boys would never attempt to drift down, for the river is still filled with drifting timbers and wrecks of houses and barns.

"And even if they should have decided to change locations, notwithstanding the peril of the undertaking, they would never have gone away without leaving some one here to notify me of the new position!"

Passing on up the bank of the bayou, searching for some sign in the darkness, Case finally came upon the rowboat which Alex. and Jule had left half concealed in a tangle of bushes in a little bay. Before him, then, lay the old house, dim in the night. He had heard the boys talk of visiting the place, and at once concluded that they were there.

He looked over the structure for lights, but saw none. Then he listened, catching in time the sounds which the two boys had noted. He crouched down in a patch of shrubbery and waited, listening for some indication of the presence of his chums.

Directly he heard a shrill scream of fright, then the bushes between his hiding-place and the house were shaken violently, and a small figure darted out, running at top speed and sending a scream into the night at every jump!

"If that isn't Mose," Case thought, "then there are two young negroes with most extraordinary calliope possibilities! He runs like the Old Scratch was after him, and has plenty of wind left to tell how scared he is!" he added.

The small figure came smashing through the shrubbery and finally landed in the thicket where Case had secreted himself. Here he stumbled over a trailing vine and fell forward on his face. Before he could regain his feet Case had him by the arm.

"Mose!" he said. "Keep quiet! You'll have all the pirates in the state steering in this direction! What is the matter?"

"Fo' de Lawd's sake leave dis nigger go!" wailed Mose. "Dar's ghostes in dat ol' house, an' dey's got de boys!"

"Are the boys in there?" demanded Case, giving the frightened lad a gentle shake to bring him back to his senses. "Where is the Rambler?"

"Ah don' know!" gasped the little negro. "Piruts don' got de boat, an' dem ghostes don' 'pear fo' dis nigger!"

"If you don't brace up and tell me what's going on," Case declared, "I'll throw you in the river. Where are the boys?"

Before Mose could reply Captain Joe came dashing through the bushes. He stopped by Case's side and lay down, trembling with excitement.

"If the dog could talk he would tell me what's going on," Case said, reprovingly, to the negro. "Where have you two been?"

Mose, evidently encouraged by the presence of the dog, told haltingly of the attack on the Rambler that morning, of his being thrown overboard, with the dog, of his day of wandering, hungry and afraid, about the old place, and of Captain Joe following the tracks of the boys to the entrance to the house.

He said that he had lain in hiding, afraid to enter, and had kept the dog quiet until it began to get dark, when he had followed Captain Joe to a window from which the sound of voices had issued. The dog had leaped in, after he had pulled away the rotten board, he said, and there he had seen Alex. and Jule, enveloped in a ghostly light, with a white ghost struggling with the dog!

The story was told with many sidelong glances at the shadows which lay heavy on the landscape, for a moon was now struggling through drifting banks of clouds.

As the boy concluded his story, often delayed by his fright, another commotion came from the grounds nearer the old house. Lights flashed from the windows and pistol shots were heard. Getting one sniff of the acrid smell of powder, Mose leaped to his feet and bounded away again. Captain Joe lifted his nose, wrinkled it in derision, and rose to meet two figures which were pounding down the broken walk toward the bayou.

"Alex.! Jule!" called Case. "What's doing?"

"Get a move on!" panted Alex. "Get to the boat! Where did that little coon go?"

"He must be somewhere near the Rocky Mountains by this time," Case replied, falling into the fast pace set by the other boys.

Very soon there were sounds of running feet behind them, and the lads redoubled their efforts to reach the boat before any one else could get to it. Now and then a bullet cut the air close to their ears, but they were not struck.

When they came to the edge of the bayou, Mose had the boat out a rod from shore, and was doing his best to row it across with one oar. The boys did not wait for him to return to the bank, but plunged into the water and waded and swam out, Alex., the last one in, giving the craft a vigorous shove as he crawled over the stern.

Without loss of a minute's time Alex. and Case took the oars and Jule seized the helm. They were soon proceeding down the bayou at a rapid rate of speed, but, fast as they were going, others were moving faster along the bank.

"Come back or we'll fill you full of air holes!" shouted one of the pursuers.

The boys might have been forced to return to the shore only for the fact that at that moment the moon's face was hidden by a mass of clouds. Taking advantage of this, and sitting as low in the boat as possible in order to avoid the bullets which were coming in their direction, the boys made for the mouth of the blind channel, and soon felt the push of the current of the Mississippi.

Before long the sounds of pursuit died out. The old mansion, which stood on the point of land between the river and the bayou, was now in darkness. When the moon came out again it stood silent and solitary in its neglected enclosure. It seemed to the lads that everything that had taken place there must be a dream!

"Now where?" Jule asked, as the boat passed a bend and the house was no longer in sight. "Do we know where we are going, any of us?"

"Where is the Rambler?" demanded Alex. "We ought to have reached it long ago."

Then, briefly, Case repeated the story told by Mose of the capture of the motor boat. There was silence for a moment, for the boys recognized the seriousness of the situation.

There was little doubt in their minds that the Rambler would be wrecked. No boat could drift down that surging river, cluttered with driftwood as it was, without meeting with disaster. And Clay was on board, bound, and helpless in case the worst happened!

"So that is how Mose and Captain Joe happened to come to the rescue," Alex. said. "The pirate threw them off the Rambler! Well, he did a good job when he did it, anyway! But how that coon did run when we made for the window he had opened!"

Mose, nestled in the bottom of the boat, stroking Captain Joe's wet head, grinned and declared that the boys had looked like ghosts.

"It is a wonder the boy and the dog were not discovered in the grounds!" Jule remarked. "I don't see how they came to keep out of sight!"

"I can tell you!" Case put in. "Mose was so afraid that the pirates would come and get him that he lay in the bushes with his face in the dead leaves! Is that right, Mose?" he asked.

Mose had to admit that he was "sho' scared white," and Captain Joe tried to explain, in perfectly good dog talk, that he wasn't frightened a bit, but only lay by Mose to help keep his courage up!

"Well, boys," Alex. said in a moment, "we've got to study out some plan to get to Clay. We can't dodge the issue by talking of something else. What shall we do?"

"I'm for going on down the river," Alex. continued. "The pirates can't run the Rambler up stream, and so we must find her if we keep on going."

"But she has nearly ten hours the start of us," urged Jule.

"I don't think they will go far, as it is risky drifting a boat down now. They will probably go far enough to get out of the zone of pursuit and then tie up, if the boat isn't wrecked before that," he added, gravely.

"That's good judgment!" Case declared.

"We're lucky if we don't get wrecked ourselves," Jule declared, swinging the boat about to avoid a mass of wreckage which lay before her. "When we come to the bend just ahead we're likely to be pushed over to the other shore. See how the current sets that way? We'll have to go some to beat it!"

The current was indeed swift and treacherous. It swept toward the east shore with almost resistless force, and the rowboat was like an eggshell in its grasp.

"Look out for the log ahead!" cried Jule, as the boat swirled around.

But there was more than one log ahead. It seemed that a whole drive of logs, or timbers, had been caught by the flood and whirled down stream.

The boys backed water, and Jule did all he could to keep out of the mass, but the current was remorseless.

The boat struck a great timber and the force of the shock and the cracking sound which followed told of an injury to the craft. Mose stood up in the boat, for water was now coming in!

"This seems to be our good-luck night!" Case grumbled, in a sarcastic tone, as the boat lurched against a great log and came near tipping over.

"There's a raft ahead, anyway!" shouted Jule. "We can ride down on that!"

"Until it takes a notion to dump us into the drink!" complained Case.

The boat filled fast, and Captain Joe mounted the prow and looked longingly toward the bobbing timber raft just ahead. From the raft he looked back to the boys.

"I reckon the dog has more sense than we have!" Alex. exclaimed. "We'll have to take to the raft, all right, so here goes."

"Wait for a bit of light!" urged Case. "The moon will be out in a second."

In the darkness which followed the boys could feel the water rising in the boat. The current was pressing the craft down against the timber raft, and the creaking of the hull proclaimed a badly wrecked boat.

"Say," Case called out, "one of you boys get out a light. We've got to make a jump right soon. This is some adventure! What?"

Jule reached for his electric, but Alex. caught his arm.

"There's a light on the Missouri bank," he said, "and it looks to me like the cabin windows of the Rambler were sending it out. Lay low in the dark and drift with the raft!"

CHAPTER VIII — FACES AT THE WINDOW

"Look here, Red," the outlaw who had been called Sam said, addressing the giant, as the Rambler struck the half-submerged tree, "we've got up against something hard!"

"We never should have put out into the river!" retorted Red. "A few more bumps like that, and to the fishes we go! Get a pole out, and see if you can push away from that consarned tree. Then we'll soon get to shore."

Sam went into the cabin, where Clay sat, side by side with the bear cub, on a bunk.

"Where's your river pole?" he demanded. "You must have something of the kind!"

"There's one in hooks at the side of the cabin," replied the boy. "If you'll cut this cord I'll help you get out of the current."

Sam leered savagely at the boy for a moment, picked up the revolver which lay on the floor not far away, put it into a pocket, and then severed the cord.

"Mind you," he said, as Clay sprang for the pole, "if you try any tricks on us we'll chuck you to the fish!"

Without paying much attention to the threat, Clay grasped the pole and ran to the prow, which was now entangled in a wilderness of branches springing from the bole of the tree the boat had struck. The boy's strength was insufficient, and Red came to his assistance. Both pried and pushed, but it seemed impossible to back the boat against the sweep of the current.

As if to make matters worse, a long timber lodged against the stern and added its weight to that of the motor boat and the running water. Sam stood looking on with a cynical smile on his hard face.

"You never can do it," he finally declared. "We'll have to let the boat drift down in company with the tree. Just our luck to strike such a snag!"

"If that limb wasn't in the way," Red asserted, "we could get the boat out. It binds on the side of the cabin."

Clay hastened into the cabin and soon returned to the prow with an axe. Both men eyed him sharply as he came forward with the keen-edged implement.

"You know what I told you!" Sam shouted, stepping toward the boy.

"Let him alone!" commanded Red. "I reckon the kid knows what he is about!"

"Now," Clay explained, addressing the big fellow, who seemed more inclined to be friendly than his companion, "if you'll stand ready with the pole, I'll get over on the trunk and cut that limb away. Then we can edge over to the shore."

"Oh, yes!" sneered Sam. "We let you off on the tree, and you go on down and call out the police at the first landing. Not for your uncle!"

"Go on," shouted Red, to Clay. "I'll steady you with the pole, and when the limb is off you give it a poke and come on board. Will you do that?"

"Sure!" answered the boy. "I have no intention of going off and leaving the Rambler! Hand me the axe when I get down on the trunk, will you?"

Without waiting for any further conversation, which was difficult because of the roaring of the river, Clay crept over the gunwale and landed on the tree, which sank lower under his weight. Then he reached for the axe, which Red promptly passed to him.

"I wouldn't get down on that tree for a thousand dollars!" cried Sam. "If he don't time himself to a second, he'll get knocked into a cocked hat by the boat when she swings loose! I'm not stuck on taking any such chances."

"That is some kid!" Red exclaimed, admiringly, as Clay chopped away at the limb. "I wish we had him with us!"

"You want to look out for him!" Sam cautioned. "He may prove to be too much of a kid for both of us, but I've got him covered, so if he tries to — —"

The limb dropped away after a few strokes with the axe, and the boat righted and swung against the trunk. The swaying of the trunk upon which Clay stood threw him into the water, but he clung to the tree and tried to work back to the boat. Sam lifted the pole to strike his unprotected head.

"May as well get rid of him now," he declared, with an ugly oath.

Red struck the would-be murderer a savage blow in the face and reached down to assist the boy to the deck. For a moment it seemed that both of them must be drawn under the boat, but the big fellow's strength won, and Clay was hauled, dripping and exhausted, up on deck. Sam eyed him malevolently and snarled.

"It will come some time!"

Red pushed the boy toward the cabin, the look on his face friendlier than ever.

"Go and get into dry clothes," he said. "Never mind what Sam says! He means all right, only he don't know how to express himself!"

The Rambler now swung off toward the shore, and Red and Sam were kept busy working wreckage out of her course. They snarled at each other as they worked, and Clay was in constant fear that Sam would play some treacherous trick on the big fellow in return for the blow he had received. The marks of the short encounter were still on his face.

Much to his relief, the Rambler was edged into calmer water next to the Missouri shore. He had no idea at that time, even, that he would lose the boat. He did not know what had become of his chums, but he believed that in some way they would be able to come to his rescue. They had never failed him.

The Rambler drifted down for some distance, leaking a little but not seriously, and was finally worked into a little bay where there was no current.

That was a long day for the boy. Several boats passed up and down on the river, and relief parties searching for flood victims were frequently seen, but Red always announced that they were in no trouble whatever when questioned.

Clay was not bound again, but was kept in the cabin, with the door closed. He could hear calls from passing boats, but did not dare make the situation known.

During the day the outlaws devoured what cooked food there was in the cabin and gave some to the boy. Once Sam lay down for a short nap. Red was not communicative, and refused to answer any questions as to his intentions regarding the Rambler.

A fine mist came down as the night shut in, but presently the moon came out, and the outlaws began discussing the advisability of proceeding on down the river.

"We can get to our landing," Sam insisted. "Once there, we can get into the bayou back of the island, where no one will think of looking for us. We must get the boat out of sight," he went on, "before reports of her capture spread along the river. Besides, the boys will be waiting for us at the shanty."

"All right," Red finally agreed. "I'm willing to take my chance on being smashed flat by a tree or floating barn."

Clay listened to the talk with interest. Somehow he began to recognize the voice of the big fellow! Where had he heard it before? Then, like a flash, the memory came to him! The man had talked with him from the river at Cairo! There is where he had heard the voice!

At that time the big fellow had been pleading for the safety of a waif who had come on board the Rambler! Both the man and the waif had disappeared when the officers had come on board. Clay wondered where the boy was, and why this outlaw had taken an interest in him. The man appeared to be kind, though his appearance and his modes of life were against him. It was all a deep mystery to the boy.

However, the giant's defense of himself, when Sam would have mistreated and, perhaps, murdered him, led Clay to believe that he was not wholly depraved. There might be some powerful motive for his adopting the life of a river outlaw.

The boy resolved, at the first opportunity, to question Red regarding the fate of the lad who had so suddenly disappeared from the boat that night. He now saw that the willingness of his companions and himself to aid the waif had led to good results, for it was this willingness which had undoubtedly caused the giant to stand between him and injury or even death. His little loaf of bread cast on the waters had returned to good purpose!

Sam seized the pole, as soon as Red agreed to his proposition to make their way down the river without delay, and began working the Rambler out into the current.

"Better wait until that mess of wreckage passes!" Red advised, as a crush of floating timbers made its appearance under the moonlight. "If we get into that bunch we'll never get out again. It will go by in a few moments."

Sam stood looking at the mass with a frown on his sullen face. He was anxious to be away for more reasons than one. The boat had undoubtedly been reported seized long before this, and every craft passing up or down would soon be looking for her. His idea was that the lads who had left the boat would soon return and report the disappearance.

He did not know, of course, that Case was at New Madrid, or on the way there, when they had attacked Clay, nor did he suspect that Alex. and Jule had fallen into the hands of a band of bandits in every way as desperate and unscrupulous as that to which he belonged.

But, aside from the question of safety, there was another matter he wished brought to a conclusion. He had been assaulted by Red, and was raging for revenge. Once in the company of his lawless fellows, his revenge might be gained!

"There is some one on that wreckage," the watchful Sam finally declared. "I saw a movement there. Good thing we are not near enough to be asked for help."

Red looked at the floating raft and shook his head.

"There is a boat lodged against the mess," he said, "but there's no one on board her, and there's no one on the raft, either."

The light of the moon was now shut out by a drive of clouds, and the two men waited for a clear sky again. When the raft was revealed they saw a white bulldog running up and down across the timbers!

"That's the brute I pitched overboard up in the bayou!" cried Sam. "I wish I had knocked him on the head. Some of those boys are not far off."

Red laughed at the idea of the boys being there, But Clay, listening with every faculty awake, had a different notion of the capabilities of his chums.

"If Captain Joe is there," the boy mused, his heart bounding with hope, "the boys are not far off! Anyway, I'll give them a chance to see the old boat once more!" he continued, reaching out and turning on the cabin lights.

Sam uttered a fierce oath as the lights flashed out on the rushing water, and made for the cabin, but Red caught him by the arm and faced him around.

"Look here!" he snarled, "if you go to making trouble for that boy I'll send your worthless hulk bobbing down to the Gulf! The lights won't hurt! We don't have to answer any calls for help that may come. Now, edge her out into the current and leave the boy to me. There's no sense in beating up the kid!"

With a word of warning to Clay, not unkindly spoken, Red switched off the cabin lights, and then went to assist Sam in getting the Rambler out into the stream. Clay heard them saying that the raft was, after all, empty of life except for the dog.

"The boat lodged against it seems to be broken," Red said, and Clay's heart went into his throat again. He feared that the boys had been caught in wreckage and drowned. The presence of the dog showed that they had been with the broken boat, he thought.

Then, while the two men worked frantically in front, Clay heard the window leading to the cabin from the stern deck cautiously pushed aside, and then the faces of Alex. and Case appeared at the opening!

CHAPTER IX—RED DECLINES TO TALK

In a moment the ray of moonlight slanting through the west window of the cabin was cut off by a floating cloud, and the faces of the two boys passed out of view. Their voices, however, came to Clay, enquiringly.

"Are you all right?" Alex. asked.

"Have you got any dry guns in there?" was Case's question.

Clay answered both questions in a whispered affirmative and moved softly toward the window. It was necessary that some definite plan of action should be agreed upon, for the lads' presence there might be discovered at any time.

"Is Jule there?" whispered Clay.

"We're all in this neighborhood!" snickered Alex., "including Mose, Teddy and Captain Joe! We came down the river in a busted boat and on a poor raft! We should have passed theRambler only for the flash of lights in the cabin. What next?"

"First," Clay answered, "I'll get the reserve weapons. One of the outlaws has my gun, but the others are in the lower drawer of the cupboard. I've been trying to get at them for a long time, but this is the first time, since I was set free of bonds, that the men have been too busy to notice me."

Clay crawled to the cupboard and secured three revolvers, held as a reserve stock.

"Now," he directed, "you boys get through the window while the ruffians are busy and the moon is out of business."

As the boys wiggled their way through the small opening, Teddy began uttering growls of joy and welcome. He pranced about the cabin, too, in spite of all Clay could do to restrain him, tipping over chairs and rattling the dishes in a great pan on the floor, where the pirates had left them after their luncheon.

And then, as if to add to the perplexities of the situation, the clouds which veiled the moon drifted away, and a slant of light shone full on the little stern deck, and on the figures grouped there. Case and Jule pulled themselves through into the cabin, but Alex. was left crouching on the outside. Clay passed him a revolver, and started to close the window.

At that moment, attracted by the unusual commotion on the inside, Sam lurched to the door and looked through the glass panel. He saw Clay at the window, and caught sight of a figure outside and called out to Red, who was still busy at the prow, trying to keep the boat out of a mass of wreckage which was coming down faster than the boat was going for the reason that it was farther out in the current.

Almost before Red could turn around, before his brain could grasp the significance of Sam's warning shout, Clay swung the door open and turned the switch which operated the prow light. In an instant the deck of the Rambler was as light as it had ever been at noon. The cabin was still in darkness, save for the light which came through the glass panel of the door.

The hands of both outlaws swung to their hips as the light flashed out, but did not bring forth the weapons carried there. Instead, they came up empty and were pushed out straight and held there. It was Clay who had given the order to keep hands out.

Clay advanced along the unsteady deck to Sam and held his gun within an inch of his crooked nose, at the same time calling to Case to come and relieve the outlaw of his weapons.

Sam's looks would have committed murder, if savage eyes and revengeful frowns could have done so, when the weapons were taken from him. Glancing hastily at Red, Clay thought he saw an amused smile lurking in the giant's eyes.

"Now, Sam," Clay said, "we've got to repair the motors and get the Rambler out of this ruck, where the leak can be repaired, so we've got no time to waste guarding a skunk like you. You would have murdered me if Red hadn't interfered, but I'm going to give you a chance for your life! Can you swim?"

"Fo' de Lawd's sake!" grunted Mose, appearing on the deck, wet and shivering from the river, "dat's de 'dentical question he done ask me!"

Captain Joe, who had come on board from the raft with the negro, sniffed at the heels of the outlaw and seemed to ask permission of Clay to take a bite out of him. The cub pranced around the little waif as if he had found a friend from whom he had long been parted. Sam did not answer the question. He glared at the weapons, at the exposed fangs of the bulldog, and turned a scowling face to Red.

"These rascals seem to be friends of yours," he said. "I don't hear anything about your being given a chance to swim! Is this a frame-up?"

Red's already flushed face darkened at the insulting question, and he would have struck Sam only that Case, whose gun was at his breast, motioned him to desist.

"There'll come a time!" growled Sam. "Me an' you will have a settlement right soon after we get shut of these imitation tramps. Understand that?"

"Yes, kiddo," Red cut in, turning to Clay, "Sam can swim. He's great on giving exhibition stunts in the water. He can do anything with water except drink it."

"Glad to know it!" Clay replied, "for I want to see how far he can swim! Take a run-and-jump, you toy pirate, and get overboard."

"Fo' de Lawd's sake, dat's what he said to dis — —"

Sam did not wait to hear the completion of the sentence, for Captain Joe, sensing, doubtless, that the outlaw was in bad with the party, advanced upon him. The pirate sprang for a floating timber, missed it, and went under. He came up in a second and struck out for the shore through a comparatively clear channel. The boys watched him until he crawled out on a mud bank and then turned to Red.

"Well?" asked that individual, a smile on his face. "What next?"

"First," Clay said, "I want to thank you for saving me from that ruffian, and then I want you to sit down and wait until we get up the greatest dinner that ever was served on the Mississippi. I'm half starved, and I know that the boys are. Of course, if you want to land right now, we'll put you ashore."

"I reckon," Red replied, with a slight tremble in his gruff voice, "that I can't do better than to stick here for a time!"

"Well," Clay went on, "the boys are wet and cold, as well as hungry, and so I'll have to do the cooking. Will you come in the cabin and sit by me while I do it?"

"Will I? I'm lucky not to be out there on the shore with Sam!"

The two passed into the cabin, after the boys had put on dry clothes and warmed themselves at the coal stove, and Clay set about cooking a mammoth steak which had been bought at Cairo and kept in the tiny refrigerator. Then he boiled potatoes, and made light biscuit, and the coffee he produced was a hearty meal in itself! There were tinned beans, and sardines, and salmon, and many other things when the meal began, but when it was over the table was bare of everything in the provision line!

In the joy and comfort of being full-fed, Mose, Captain Joe, and Teddy rolled up in a common rug on the floor, in a corner where they would not be in the way, and went to sleep. Clay and Red went out on deck while the others washed the dishes.

"Are you thinking of sticking about this section all night?" asked the latter.

"Only for a short time," Clay answered. "We'll fix the motors, directly, and go on down the river. Why do you ask the question? Don't you want to stay here?"

"I was thinking," Red observed, quite coolly, "that, with the lights going, and the shore not far away, Sam might be thinking of taking a shot or two at the boys!"

"But he hasn't any gun!" Clay exclaimed.

"Yes, he has," Red returned. "He has a gun that wasn't found on him. He keeps it in a watertight sack under his left arm. He's used to taking to the water!"

"And you think he will hang about the bank, walking down from where he was put off, and try to pick us off?" asked Clay. "How far are we now from the mud bank he mounted?"

"Not more than a couple of miles," was the reply. "We are in water that shows only a trace of current now, because there is a great headland just below, and the flood has packed the curve full. He probably has been able to keep up with the boat."

"That isn't going very fast!" laughed Clay, "for it has been at least two hours since he left the boat. The moon, which is in the first quarter, sets about eleven, and it is hiding itself in the trees already!"

"I wouldn't advise sticking hereabouts," insisted Red. "I can say no more!"

"All right!" Clay replied. "We'll fix the motors and start on down. Here, Case," he called out, "did you bring the repairs?"

"Surest thing you know!" was the answer, and in a short time Clay was at work on the motive power, which was not much out of repair and was soon fixed.

"You know, of course," Clay said to Red, as the Rambler, under perfect control, started down stream at a pace which kept the driftwood from lunging against her stern, "that I recognize you as the man who talked with me out of the river at Cairo?"

"I never suspected it!" was the slow reply. "How do you know I'm the man?"

"Your voice!" was the reply. "It puzzled me at first, though."

"I'll have to trade voices with some river rascal!" grinned Red.

"You spoke, that night, about a boy who had come on board?" Clay said, tentatively.

"That was my business there," Red replied, with a slight frown.

"Where did the boy go that night? We never saw him after the officers came on board. He must have swum to the Missouri shore."

"He did," was the hesitating reply. "He made it, too!"

"Why didn't he remain with us?" asked Clay.

"He got scared! If I had kept away he might have done so."

"Is he your son?" was the next question Clay asked.

Red looked the boy in the face steadily for a moment and then asked:

"You don't want to harm the lad, do you?"

"I want to help him," was the reply. "He looked so forlorn, and wet, and cold, and hungry, that I've thought of him a lot since. Where is he now?"

"Well," Red said, in a perplexed tone, "that is what I can't tell you."

"Because you don't know where he is?" demanded Clay.

"No; not that. I know where he is, but I can't tell you."

"Is the child implicated in any crime?" Clay asked, looking sharply into the man's flushed face. "Is there any reason why he can't go with us?"

"Why do you suggest crime in connection with the kid?" demanded Red, a frown on his face. "He may be associated with criminals, innocently, and yet be worthy of all your confidence and esteem!"

They talked a long time about the boy, about the events of the day, and about the future plans of the Rambler boys. The boat made good progress during the night while all save Clay and his strange companion slept. With the first flush of dawn Red asked to be put ashore, refusing to give any reason for wanting to leave the boat.

"You've used me mighty white," he said at parting, "and there'll come another day! Don't you ever forget that, lads! There'll come another day! And if you come across that waif again, just feed him, and warm him, and clothe him, and pass him on to wherever he wants to go. Thank you all!" and he was gone!

"What do you think of that for a mystery?" Clay asked as the man disappeared in a grove near the landing. "We shall hear from Red again."

CHAPTER X— MORE RIVER OUTLAWS

"And I have a notion that we'll run across that waif again," Case said. "I imagine that he is somewhere down the river, and that Red will not be far away when we come to him. Somehow, we bunt into mysteries wherever we go!"

"I've got a hunch," Alex. exclaimed, "that we are headed for news of that warehouse robbery at Rock Island! It seems to me too, that the boy had something to do, with it, or is mixed up in it in some way."

"He looked pretty lean and shabby for a chap who had been interested in a diamond robbery!" Jule suggested. "Perhaps he's not guilty — just suspected!"

The day was fine and the flood was running out. The river showed less wreckage than had been seen the day before, for the lowering water caused much of it to land on headlands and sandbars. During the forenoon the Rambler, which was still leaking a trifle, passed several river shanties and houseboats, tied up below half-submerged islands, where they were protected from wreckage.

These houseboats are common all along the Ohio, Cumberland, Tennessee and Mississippi rivers. Fishermen and indolent river characters live in them the year round. Some of the boats are of good size and well built and furnished, while others are merely shanties built on rafts of logs and other spoils taken from the waters.

Many of the boats carry whole families, and go sailing toward the Gulf with streamers of shirts and petticoats blowing from clotheslines. Others carry two or three men and numberless dogs. Those who reside on the boats live principally on fish, and on corn meal and pork purchased with the proceeds of fish sales.

Shortly after dinner the boys were asked to come on board a shanty boat navigated by two men and numerous dogs, so the Rambler was run alongside and Clay and Alex. went aboard, where they were warmly welcomed by two Chicago young men who were making the river trip in the way of a winter vacation. Their quarters were crude but comfortable. They had had a rough voyage because of the flood, but declared that they were going down to the Gulf if the raft held out.

Almost the first question Clay asked was about the Rock Island robbery.

"So you have been overhauled by the officers, too, have you?" laughed one of the young men, called Ben by his chum. "We had a bit of that, also, but the officers didn't remain with us very long. It doesn't take a week to search our craft!"

"Are you sure they were officers?" asked Clay.

"Oh, yes, they were officers, all right. They asked for a boy of about twelve, who, they declared, had been seen down the river, and who is believed to have been associated with the Rock Island robbers. They also asked for a man of six feet and over, with red hair."

Clay looked at Alex. significantly and asked for any news they might have of the robbery—any details they might have learned.

"Oh, we got the story from a St. Louis newspaper we begged of a steamer captain," was the reply. "It seems that the silks, furs, and diamonds stolen were stored in the warehouse one day and taken out by thieves that same night. A boy answering to the description of the one the officers asked for was seen about the premises during the afternoon, and at one time he was observed in the company of a giant of a man with red hair.

"It is the theory of the police that the thieves captured the boy and forced him to enter through a broken window and unfastened the door, à~la Oliver Twist. They believe that if he can be caught he will be able to identify the robbers if they are caught. The red-headed man was seen in the city, wandering about the streets, aimlessly, on the night of the crime. It is not believed that he was interested in the robbery personally. However, they want him because he seemed to take a great interest in the boy."

"Have the officers found any of the stolen property?" asked Alex.

"Not that we know of," was the reply. "The robbers got off handily, and it is believed they put the goods on board some river boat and sent them down toward New Orleans. Diamonds, silks and furs can be hidden in a small space."

The boys visited with the strangers for an hour or more and then went on down the river, sailing a very little faster than the shanty boat, which depended entirely on the current, and which was obliged to tie up at intervals to avoid wreckage.

"I've got a notion," Alex. said, as the boys left the shanty boat in the distance, "that the newspaper story is the right one. That boy never took part in that robbery of his own free will, though. I am sure of it! And the man? That was Red he described, eh?"

"It undoubtedly was," Clay replied, thoughtfully.

"That's your bosom friend!" Alex. grinned. "You let him escape!"

"What else could I do, under the circumstances?" demanded Clay. "The fellow saved my life! Sam would have murdered me only for him!"

"Well, if he's on the level, what's he doing with a man like Sam?" questioned Alex., still grinning.

"We shall have to leave that question to the future," was the short reply.

"You believe that Red had a hand in the robbery at Rock Island?" persisted the boy.

"I don't think anything about it! I'm waiting for additional information!"

"Well, we've got a long way to go yet," Case cut in, "and we may meet with the red-headed man again. We may meet him in some jail yet, if our luck doesn't change!"

"Speaking about jails," Alex. questioned, "what do you make of the old jail of a house Jule and I were locked up in? What do you think they wanted to hold us for?"

"Probably to keep you from spying on what was going on there," Clay suggested.

"But what was going on there?" asked Alex. "That is what we didn't find out!"

"Whatever it was," Jule observed, "the people interested in keeping it secret took long chances when they left us in the dark room with only an old man to guard us. And imagine them never knowing that Mose and the dog were in the grounds!"

At mention of Mose Alex. burst into a roar of laughter.

"I never saw a human face that showed real fear until I saw Mose looking in at the broken window!" he said, directly. "I have seen men and women show fright, but never anything like that! He thought he had come on a collection of ghosts! I presume he thought we, Jule and I, were dead and buried in the cellar, and that our spirits had come forth to haunt the murderers! And he streaked it away like a flash of light!"

"There's probably nothing worse than the manufacture of moonshine whisky going on in the old house," Case contributed. "Or the loot from the warehouse may have been stored there," he added. "The boys heard heavy articles being moved, though they may have been scared stiff and mistook the footsteps of a mouse for the heavy noises!"

"I hope you'll get in just such a predicament some day!" growled Jule. "It wasn't any fun, sitting there in the dark! And I expected that crazy old man to shoot us any moment! I believe he was crazy! He acted as if he was!"

"That's right!" exclaimed Case. "Keep on talking, and I won't have to wash a dish all the way to the Gulf. I love to hear you get funny."

"That will do for you!" cried Jule, gleefully. "I see you washing the supper dishes right now!"

"I'd like to go back and investigate that old house," Alex. observed. "It would be great fun! I believe it stood there when the cave-dwellers lived along the Chickasaw bluffs, and that was before De Soto discovered the river and was buried in its depths."

"I thought La Salle discovered the Mississippi," Case said, with a wink at Clay.

"He made a stab at navigating it from the Illinois river down," Alex. answered, seeing that Case was prodding him in the desire of receiving information. "But he gave the wrong course to the stream. The real Mississippi turns at St. Louis and runs off toward the Rocky Mountains."

"Yes it does!" exclaimed Jule. "You're in need of mental rest, young man."

"Certainly it does," Alex. insisted. "The longest stretch of water takes the river name, doesn't it? Well, the Missouri is about three thousand miles long from the fountain-heads of the Gallatin, Madison and Red Rock lakes to the junction with the Mississippi, while from the junction to headwaters the Mississippi is only about twelve hundred miles long!"

"It does seem as if the longest river should carry the name," said Case. "In that event, this would be the Missouri river!"

"Sure it would," insisted Alex. "The river from the Red Rock lakes to the Gulf is the longest river in the world — eight hundred miles longer than the Amazon, though not so wide! Some day the name of the Missouri will become the Mississippi, or the Mississippi will be called the Missouri!"

The boys argued over the proposition for a long time, until it was time to get supper, and then Clay and Alex. began watching for ducks, with which the river swarms at times. While they secured three fair-sized birds, Alex. caught fish, and insisted on their being cooked with the ducks.

"I'll never get enough to eat if I leave the menu to you boys," he declared, "and Mose feels about it just as I do!" he added, pulling the little negro's ear.

"Ah sure do feel empty!" answered Mose, rolling up his eyes.

The Mississippi is a tangle of channels and islands above Memphis, and the boys decided to tie up for the night on the down-stream side of one of the little "tow-heads" which are so frequently seen close to larger islands. These are formed by deposits of sand and vegetable matter, but they increase in size rapidly as soon as cotton-wood brush takes possession of the new ground, assisting materially in resisting the encroachments of the current.

The islands of the Mississippi are numerous and uncertain as to location. They have all been formed by the cutting of new channels across headlands. The river itself winds like a very crooked snake through the soft bottom lands of the south, and the water is forever finding new and shorter ways to reach the Gulf.

From the junction of the Ohio, there are one hundred and twenty-five numbered islands from Cairo to Bayou la Fourche, in Louisiana, and besides these there are nearly as many more which bear the names of the owners. Many of these islands are grown up with impenetrable thickets or show only deserted fields.

In proceeding down the great river the boys had kept on only sufficient power to gain steerway, as they were in no haste to reach the Gulf of Mexico, which was their final destination on that trip. They decided that day to travel nights no more.

After supper had been eaten the boys switched on all the lights and sat out on deck. There was a brilliant moon, but they preferred to let everybody in that vicinity know that they were there—hence the electric lights.

"If any one sneaks up on us now," Alex. laughed, "he'll have to get to us by the under-water route! And, even then, one of us would be apt to see him. Captain Joe is losing his record as a watch dog, but I guess Teddy can take his place."

Captain Joe, as if he understood every word that had been said, and resented the insinuation, walked up to the prow and sat in a meditative mood, looking over the small "tow-head" which sheltered the boat from the current. He sat there motionless so long that Alex. finally called attention to him.

"Ah knows what he's done seein'!" exclaimed Mose. "Dar's a big fat coon watchin' us from dat mess ob bushes. Ah done seen him long time ago!"

An inspection of the spot pointed out showed half a dozen evil-looking negroes watching the boat.

CHAPTER XI — FIRE-FACES ON THE ISLAND

"What are they squatting there watching the boat for?" queried Jule, as the prow light fell full on the group of negroes on the island. "They don't look good to me!"

"If we keep away from them," Case suggested, "and don't try to stare them out of countenance, they'll probably keep away from us. They do look fierce, though!"

While the boys discussed the matter the negroes moved away from the shore of the island, where they were under the boat lights, and secreted themselves behind a patch of willows which fringed the "tow-head," for the place where they were was little else.

"I don't believe they have any idea of letting us alone, if they can manage to get on board the Rambler," Clay declared. "I have often read that lawless negroes and whites are alike alert for plunder during flood seasons, and it is floating goods those fellows are after, unless I am much mistaken. We'll have to keep a sharp watch to-night."

"Wouldn't it be wiser to drive them away?" asked Alex., with one of his grins.

"We have no right to drive them away," Case suggested. "We may get into trouble if we try it. I'll watch half the night and not mind it at all."

Alex. nudged Jule in the side and whispered in his ear for a moment.

"Jule and I will watch the first half," he then said. "Perhaps they will go off home by midnight, and Case won't have to watch at all."

"Alex.," Clay exclaimed, "you've got some mischief in your mind. Heretofore you've come out of your scrapes with whole bones, but sometime you'll get into serious trouble if you don't stop running out nights. I strongly advise you to let those levee negroes alone! You go to bed early, and I'll watch the boat!"

"Who's got mischief in the mind?" grinned Alex. "I guess I can stay up until midnight without gettin' into trouble! You see if I don't make the dandy watchman to-night! When it comes to keeping guard, I'm the candy boy!"

"You usually manage to get into trouble when you are left alone!" laughed Clay.

"If I can't be good to-night," grinned Alex., "I'll be careful."

Nothing more was seen of the negroes at that time, although the boys were satisfied that they were still on the island, as no boat had been seen to leave it.

After a time Clay, Case and Mose went to bed, leaving Alex., Jule, Captain Joe, and Teddy on deck. The dog seemed particularly wide awake, moving about as if he scented danger, while the cub sat looking toward the island with twitching nostrils.

"Seems as if the dog and the cub know there's something coming off here to-night," Jule remarked, as Captain Joe put his paw on the gunwale and sniffed the air. "Do you really think they have a way of discovering approaching peril which human beings have not? Captain Joe certainly looks as if he saw something unpleasant coming."

"I often think dogs have an instinct which warns them of danger," Alex. replied.

"Well," Jule went on, "we'll soon see what comes of the signals of danger he is now handing out to us! Whatever he sees or senses is on that island."

The boys watched for a long time, but there came no sounds of life from the island.

"You're like the dog," Jule said to Alex., presently. "You are getting ready for a break of some sort! Suppose you loosen up and tell me what it is?"

"You remember that night on the Amazon, when we scared the life out of a couple of renegade Englishmen and a native Indian?" asked Alex.

"Sure I do!" was the reply. "That was the funniest ever!"

"Well," Alex. explained, "I'm goin' to try something like that on these negroes."

"Better let 'em alone!" advised Jule. "They are wise to tricks!"

"Shucks!" Alex. laughed. "I'll have them walking on their heads, and walking the water at that. I wish I had a boat, so I wouldn't have to swim to the island!"

"We've lost a rowboat every trip!" Jule exclaimed. "I wonder why we didn't pick the one we had off the raft and fix it up. It wasn't badly smashed."

"We may find it yet," Alex. said, hopefully. "We have come down just a little faster than the current, and so it is probably behind us. When it comes down we'll get it and make it as good as new."

"Yes, when we get it!" laughed Jule. "There's a thousand people along the island beaches and mainland levees watching for boats! Just like these negroes are watching for anything at all that seems worth picking out of the water!"

"It won't do any harm to keep a lookout for it," Alex. decided. "Now," he added, turning out the lights and throwing off his coat, "do you want to go to the shore with me? If you will go I'll show you a race that will beat anything you ever saw."

"And leave the boat alone?" demanded Jule. "I should say not. I'll remain here and see that your retreat is properly covered. You'll want some one here to hold a gun on the negroes you seem determined to stir up."

"Now don't get a grouch on," pleaded Alex. "I'm doing this purely in the interest of science! I want to see how far the emancipation proclamation has relieved the negroes of the south from the old-time superstitions of the race! Not to put too fine a point upon it, kid, I want to see what a good healthy ghost will do to a lot of river thieves! Do you get me?"

"Going to play ghost, are you," laughed Jule. "Then I'll be a ghost, too!"

Alex. listened at the cabin door for a moment, but heard no sounds indicating the lack of sleep on the inside. Then he crept in, fumbled around in the darkness until he found two old bathing suits and a square package which smelled of sulphur.

"Now," he explained to Jule, as he came out, "we'll put on these bathing suits, so as to have dry clothes ready when we return from the island! You take a part of the matches, for we may become separated in the thicket. We won't do the Mephisto act until we get to the island, then rub the sulphur on thick — on your hands and face."

"I guess I know how!" Jule remonstrated.

The boys placed their clothing in two piles on the deck and donned the bathing suits — much to the wonder of Captain Joe, who wrinkled his nose and looked suspiciously at the boys. His remarks on the subject of bathing in a swift river in the night time were not in favor of the experiment. However, he crouched down by Alex.'s feet and expressed himself as willing to share in the doubtful expedition.

"When we get into the willows," Alex. explained, "I'll let out a yell which will put Mose's efforts in that direction away to the bad! Then you run at them on the right and I'll close in on the left, and we'll see a race that will put the Greek events out on a blind siding with fires banked. When you are ready, drop in and swim for the bunch of willows straight ahead. Swim slow and don't make any noise."

The boys left the dark deck of the Rambler and entered the water. There was little current where the boat lay, and they had no difficulty in making the willows pointed out by the promoter of the midnight excursion. The lights of Memphis made a faint haze in the sky to the south. The wash of the river drowned all individual noises. In the distance the caving of a bank sent down a heavy sound.

Believing that they had left the boat without awakening any of the sleepers and landed on the island without attracting the attention of the negroes, the boys crouched down in a thicket and listened.

The moon, which would set about midnight, was low down in the west, and gave a fitful light at rare intervals. There was a heavy mass of thunderheads in the sky, and few stars showed through. There were no indications of a light or fire on the island.

The boys, however, were much mistaken in their understanding of the situation. When they dropped off the deck of the Rambler, Clay poked his head out of the cabin and watched them as far as the darkness would permit. Then he returned to the cabin, put on a bathing suit and took a square box from the cupboard.

The box contained the reserve weapons and flashlights of the party and was waterproof. With this in his hand, and leaving Captain Joe on guard, with strict orders not to leave the deck, he entered the water and swam toward the shore, turning away from the bunch of willows where the two boys had landed.

Of course he did not know that Alex. and Jule had left the water there, but it seemed to him that they would naturally select the nearest point as their landing place. Once on shore he sat down to await developments.

He was certain that Alex. and Jule had entered upon a dangerous expedition. The river negroes of the south are by no means as superstitious as is generally believed, and Clay knew it. He doubted if they would run far at sight of a face blazing with sulphur. It was his opinion that the boys would be the ones to start the race!

The negroes were sure to be armed, and they might be drunk, in which case they would not be likely to permit the outer spirits to bluff the inner spirits! Besides, they might have valuable plunder on the island, and some would be brave enough to remain and fight for it.

Of course, if Clay had gravely asked the boys to give over their proposed joy visit to the island, they would undoubtedly have done so, but he did not care to do that. His thought was that he ought not to attempt to control the actions of he boys, as they all stood equal on the trip, no one having authority over the others.

Besides, if the truth must be told, Clay, himself, was not averse to a little excitement! In addition, he was anxious to know what was doing on the island, and why the negroes were assembled there.

Another feature of the situation was that a watcher on the beach saw all three forms in the water as they left the boat! When the lads landed,

Alex. and Jule at the clump of willows and Clay farther to the west, this watcher lost no time in communicating with his fellows in their rough-and-ready camp near the center of the little "tow-head."

The noise made by the negroes in getting ready to meet whatever attack might be made upon them gave the location of their camp to Clay, and he pressed as close to it as it was possible for him to do without advancing into the open, where he might have been seen during any moment of moonlight.

It was a chill night, and there was a wind blowing from the west which seemed to cut into his bones, but Clay sat down not far from the camp and awaited the opening of the drama! He could hear the campers moving about, but could not distinguish the words spoken. The moon sank out of sight for good before any movement was made.

Then Clay saw a figure fit to frighten the most courageous leave the fringe of willows and advance deliberately toward the center of the island. He had hard work to make himself understand that the thing he saw was only one of the boys. If the very Old Scratch himself had set foot on the "tow-head" he could not have presented a more sinister appearance. Clay watched the advance of the figure with bated breath.

In a second after the figure appeared, flaming of face and pointing hands, with a great cross of fire on what appeared to be a naked breast, a long, wavering cry went up from the camp, and then there came a rush of feet. Clay could not tell at first which way the feet were going, but a moment convinced him that they were putting a swift distance between the camp and the devil-figure approaching.

When a second figure, marked like the first, appeared the shrieks of alarm, the running of frightened feet, were drowned by the commands of a bull-like voice to stop the panic-stricken flight and use revolver and knife!

CHAPTER XII — HALF FULL OF DIAMONDS

At that moment, notwithstanding the commotion and the threats of coming trouble, Clay felt like congratulating Alex. and Jule on the manner in which they were carrying out their reckless plans. More blood-curdling shrieks than now proceeded from the throats of the boys he had never heard.

Knowing that defeat, perhaps death, would instantly follow on the heels of retreat, Alex. and Jule charged the camp, swinging their fire-coated arms and uttering cries which it did not seem possible could issue forth from human lips. There naturally followed a swifter flight on the part of the negroes.

But three or four black men, less superstitious, or having more at stake, than the others, stood their ground, calling to their companions that it was a white man's trick, and that they should return and ascertain by the use of steel and lead just how human their visitors were. For a time the voices of the courageous ones did not check the mad rush for the river, but finally a group gathered on the beach and engaged in conversation, which, of course, Clay could not hear.

Alex. and Jule now "disappeared" in approved "ghost" fashion — that is, they drew black cloths over their faces and hands so that their flaming make-up could no longer be seen. In fact, it was now so dark, the moon having set, that even the figures of the boys could not be seen when they crouched on the ground. The negroes on the beach were only visible because they formed quite a large group and kept constantly in excited motion.

Clay wondered if the boys would now understand that their trick had failed and make for the Rambler. At the first rush the negroes had fled, but they were now listening to arguments intended to reassure them, and the ultimate result was not in doubt.

Before long the black men would swarm back to the camp, perhaps make a thorough search of the entire "tow-head," in which case the boys were sure to be discovered, unless they made their way back to the boat before the search began. Clay placed himself between the camp and the boat and waited, thinking that his reserve weapons might be needed.

The information that he had seen figures leaving the boat just before the advent of the "ghosts," as given by the watcher, had instant effect on the negroes. They swarmed back toward the camp, making a great many more threats than Clay thought was necessary! Two familiar figures now came dashing toward Clay, and he called out softly to them to halt a moment. The figures developed into two rather frightened boys as soon as they came close to the watcher.

"Me for the boat!" panted Jule. "I reckon these coons know a ghost when they see one—not! Me for the feathers, too when I light! Come on, Alex!"

"Go on and get aboard!" Alex. urged. "I want to see Clay a moment."

Jule darted away and was soon out of sight. Although he had carefully made up as a disciple of Old Nick, he was careful not to exhibit any of his trade-marks as he moved towards the boat! Clay and Alex. stood listening to the commotion for a moment, and then the latter panted, taking Clay's arm as he did so, and drawing him back toward the camp:

"When I got up there," he said, "I stumbled over some one lying on the ground! I felt about for a minute and found pretty much rags! Then some one told me to get off the island or I would be murdered."

"Go on!" Clay said excitedly. "We have no time to lose if we are to investigate this matter. Was the person you talked with a prisoner?"

"Sure he was. He asked me to cut the cords, but I had no knife with me and so had to make an effort to untie them. The captive talked while I was at work on the knots, and who do you think it was. Give you three guesses!"

"Hurry! Hurry! We have no time to lose, I tell you, if the captive is in need of our assistance. Who is it?"

"The kid who came on board the Rambler at Cairo!" replied Alex.

"And you had to leave him there—tied?"

"What else could I do?" asked Alex. "I didn't have even a knife! This foolish bathing suit has no pockets, so I brought no arms with me. What could I do, when the coons were making a rush for the camp?"

"We've got to get that kid!" Clay cried.

"If they would only go away for a minute," Alex. declared, "I could get him and bring him to the boat, ropes and all!"

A shot came from the Rambler, and, turning, the boys saw that the craft was aglow with electric lights! Instantly they crouched lower in the willows, for the strong prow lamp cast a ray far over on the "tow-head."

Another shot came from the boat, and then the negroes at the camp made a break for the beach, passing within a rod of where the two boys lay concealed.

"Shall we take them in the rear?" asked Alex. "They have attacked the boat."

"Don't shoot!" warned Clay. "Remember that we had no right to molest them in the first place! The boys on the boat are awake, or the lights wouldn't be on. They can protect themselves, I reckon. I hope Jule is in a safe place!"

The lights were still on, but not a person could be seen. Then more shots came, and Clay saw that the boys were firing through the small port holes in the gunwale, and that the negroes were contenting themselves with firing volley after volley at the cabin windows, which were now void of glass!

While the boys on shore watched with intense anxiety, the motors of the Rambler were heard, and then the boat began to drop down stream.

"I wonder if Jule got on board?" Alex. asked.

"If he met with no opposition on the way he probably did," was the reply. "At least we must suppose that he is either on the boat or in hiding on the island."

"Come on, then!" shouted Alex. "We'll make a success of this excursion yet. We'll take possession of the camp. I want a confidential talk with the prisoner!"

"You'll be getting a confidential talk with a bullet pretty soon, if you don't pay more attention to getting off!" Clay answered. "The boat has dropped down, and the negroes will soon be back here. It is another swim! What?"

Almost before Clay had done speaking Alex. was off in the darkness. Clay could just see his figure moving along the ground, so he followed on after him, wondering what new trick the lad had in mind. The light from the Rambler grew fainter every instant. For some reason unknown to Clay, the boat was being moved down stream a long way.

In a moment Clay saw Alex. bending over a figure lying on the ground at the edge of a rude windbreak of willow bushes, cut and woven together.

"Where's the coon's boat?" he asked, hurriedly.

Clay smiled happily. He had not thought of that!

"Off there on the east side," replied the boy. "Have you got a knife yet?"

For answer Alex. seized the lad by the feet and called out to Clay:

"Catch him by the shoulders, and we'll carry him!"

Clay was not slow in following the suggestion, and the boys soon had the captive between the fringe of willows and the water. The boat was there, a large, four-oared craft which was partly filled with plunder taken from the river. The negroes were evidently making a business of gathering supplies from the flood. Just then Jule came up, out of breath from a stumbling run in the dark.

The captive was placed on board, and then Clay seized a pair of heavy oars.

"Take the helm," he called to Alex., "and you help with the oars, Jule," he added.

Then the craft shot out into the current. When she came around the corner of the little island, where the light from the Rambler struck her a series of frantic shouts came from the men huddled on the south bank, and a few shots were fired, but, the current running swiftly, they were soon out of range.

"Let 'em swim," chuckled Alex. "A bath will be good for what ails them!"

"Alex.," remarked Clay, panting with the heavy work at the oars, "you deserve a Carnegie medal!"

"Sure!" chuckled the other. "I'm the Johnny-on-the-Spot when it comes to prescribing healthful stunts for the working classes! Where is that boat going?" he added as the Ramblerdisappeared around a distant bend in the stream.

"This is what comes of running off in the night without telling the boys what we were up to!" panted Jule. "This is some boat, when it comes to weight."

In ten minutes the lights of the Rambler were in sight again, the rowboat having passed around the bend. Then Clay took out a searchlight and began making signals to those on board. Directly an answering signal came from the boat, and then the lights halted, turned, and came up stream.

"You're a nice lot of watchmen!" Case called out, as the two boats came close together. "We thought you had caught a floater boat and drifted down stream."

"This," grinned Alex., "is the only old and original relief expedition. We have with us to-night a brand snatched from the coons!"

"Hand down a knife!" called Clay. "This lad is capable of climbing on board by his own self! And swing around a little so as not to tip us over!"

With no little difficulty the boys were landed on the deck of the Rambler. Case regarded the visitor with a quizzical smile as he bent over him.

"Did you take a dive at Cairo," he asked, "and come up at Memphis?"

The boy answered only by a weary smile, and Mose stood staring at him with widening eyes, while Captain Joe sniffed suspiciously at his worn garments. Teddy invited him to a boxing match!

"I'll go you boys a dollar to an apple," Case observed, "that this kid is still empty! He looks it! Anyway, I'll go and get him something to eat!"

"And don't forget the heroic rescuers!" Alex. called out. "I haven't had a thing to eat since supper! Say, kid," he went on, "what's your name?"

"Chester Vinton," was the reply, in a frightened voice. "I'm running away."

"You wasn't running very fast when we found you!" commented Alex. "How did you come to mix with those wreckers?"

"I was on a raft," was the answer, "and I was hungry, and I saw them on the island, and asked them for something to eat. They tied me up!"

"Why didn't you stay on board the boat at Cairo?" asked Clay.

"I was afraid," was the reply.

"Red is back up the river looking for you," Jule observed, still shivering from his exposure to the cold water. "He took passage with us part of the way down."

"I should think he did!" chuckled Alex. "And he was a first cabin passenger at that!"

"Well," Clay decided, presently, "perhaps we'd better feed this boy and put him to bed. He looks as if he'd been up against something hard."

The lad ate ravenously, and then began undressing. Clay sat in the cabin with him. He was full of wonderment at this second meeting with the boy, and wanted to ask him a hundred questions, but decided to wait until the lad was in better condition.

As the visitor threw his ragged clothes off a thud on the floor told of something of considerable weight in one of the pockets.

"Do you carry a gun, lad?" he asked, stooping over to lift the trousers.

The boy bounded forward and snatched at the trousers, but Clay was too quick for him. The article which had made the noise on the floor was a leather bag.

An investigation showed that it was half full of diamonds of exceptional quality!

CHAPTER XIII — A RIVER ROBBER IN A NEW ROLE

With half a dozen stones of splendid value rolling over the palm of his hand, Clay regarded the boy accusingly.

"Where did you get the diamonds?" he asked.

The boy did not answer. Clay had expected confusion and shame. Instead he met with anger and reproach. Chester ("Chet" from that day forward) shot forward like an arrow and tried to wrest the bag from his hands. Clay put him back tolerantly.

"Give them back to me!" Chet shouted so loudly that the boys out on the deck entered the cabin and stood in an astonished group about the two.

Clay, grasping the bag and the lose gems, held his hands high above his head.

"Where did you get them?" he persisted.

"Give them back to me!" yelled Chet. "You've been following me for this, have you? You're all as bad as the river thieves I've met up with! Give them to me!"

"What do you think of the little one for a diamond dip?" asked Alex., pointing at the flushed face of the agitated boy. "He's some clever!"

"I reckon he belongs with Red, the Robber, all right!" Jule put in.

"He seems to be pretty well fixed!" laughed Case. "Those gems are worth more than a hundred thousand dollars! Did you swipe them from the men who robbed the Rock Island warehouse, kid?" he added.

Chet turned a flaming face toward this new accuser.

"Don't you dare call me a thief!" he shouted. "The diamonds are mine! I never stole them. Give them back to me, you — you — river pirates!"

"That's good, coming from him!" grinned Alex. "Come on, little one, and tell us who these stones belong to."

"I tell you they are mine!" Chet again insisted. "I never stole them! You give them back to me! If I had the strength I'd tear your heart out!"

"Of course!" laughed Clay. "Of course you'd do something desperate if you had the strength! But don't trouble yourself about the diamonds! If they belong to you, you shall have them. But we don't want to harbor a thief, you know!"

"I don't believe you'll ever give them back to me!" sobbed the boy. "I've brought them down the river, all this way, to be robbed of them at last!"

In a spasm of grief the lad threw himself on the cabin floor and burst into an uncontrollable fit of weeping. The boys stood around for a moment, looking rather sheepishly at each other, and then all left the cabin but Clay.

"Come kid," the latter said, lifting Chet from the floor and holding him in his arms like a baby, "don't act like you'd lost your last friend! If you're honest, you've found friends instead of losing them. You shall have the diamonds back, if you can show that they belong to you. Brace up, now, and go on to bed!"

Chet regarded Clay through wet eyes for a moment and then slipped away to the bunk which had been set aside for him. The frank inspection seemed to have in a measure restored his equanimity. Clay sat down by the side of the bunk, the diamonds in his hands.

"Why don't you tell me all about it?" he asked of the boy. "Why not settle the whole matter right here, and so have done with it? Where did you get them?"

"I've promised not to tell," was the reply.

"You are not making a very good beginning," Clay admonished.

Chet made no reply whatever, but turned his face away. Clay went on, patiently:

"Where is your home?"

"I haven't got any home," was the reply. "I never had one."

"But you must belong somewhere," Clay insisted. "Where did you live last?"

"I'm not going to tell you anything at all," Chet replied, "until I see the man that made me promise to keep silent, and until he gives me leave to talk with you."

"Is the man you mention Red, the riverman?" asked Clay.

"Didn't I just tell you that I wasn't going to talk?" demanded the boy.

"All right," Clay responded. "Take all the time you want! In the meantime, I'll keep the diamonds. Will you promise to remain on the boat?"

"If I had the diamonds, I'd quit you right now!" said the boy, savagely. "I may as well tell you the truth. If you keep the diamonds, I'll stay until I get them, but I'll find them and take them with me if I can. You just mind that!"

"You're a frank little chap, anyway!" laughed Clay.

"I wasn't brought up to tell lies!" was the astonishing reply.

"Who brought you up?" asked Clay. "You just said you never had any home!"

"Never did!" was the reply. "Say, you won't blame me if I find where you put the diamonds and run off with them, will you?" he added, quite gravely.

"I don't see how I can blame you, after such fair warning," laughed Clay.

"And you won't help any one to find me?" persisted the little fellow.

"No," answered Clay, "if you are sharp enough to get the diamonds away from me, I'll never let on that I ever saw or heard of you. Is that satisfactory to you?"

"Will you shake hands on that?" asked Chet, sitting up on the bunk.

"Gladly! Now, go to sleep and wake up in a more communicative mood to-morrow."

"I'll stick to what I said!" Chet answered, and Clay left him alone in the cabin. When he reached the deck he was at once surrounded by the boys, all eager to know the outcome of the conference. Clay told them of what had taken place.

"He's a nervy little chap!" Clay concluded, "and I like him very much already."

"You bet he's all right, that kid!" Alex. said. "If he wasn't, he wouldn't have told you that he would get the gems the first time he got a chance. Besides, see how he is keeping the promise made to some other fellow! Where are you going to keep the diamonds, Clay?" the boy continued. "Don't you ever think the kid won't try hard to find them! I hope he won't feel called upon to cut all our throats in order to obtain possession of them! I believe he would do it if he thought it necessary!"

"Well," Clay answered, speaking in a low tone and looking in through the glass panel of the cabin door to see that Chet was still in his bunk, "I think I'll go ashore at Memphis, for supplies, you know, and put the gems in a deposit box at one of the banks."

"That's a fine idea!" cried Case. "He'll never get them there!"

"But you want to look out that you're not pinched in the bank," Alex. advised. "That warehouse robbery is making some noise, and if a boy from a river boat is seen to have diamonds, it is the jail house for yours!"

"If you put them in a bank deposit box," Jule observed, "you'd better do them up so as to look like a package of papers — bonds, or stocks, or something like that."

"That is a good idea, too!" Clay exclaimed. "I'll do it!"

"I'd give a lot to know more about the boy and the diamonds," Clay mused, as the boys began getting breakfast.

They had talked so long, after reaching the boat, that they had not before realized that it was most morning, and now there was a flush in the east which told of sunrise.

When Clay went back into the cabin to see about the fire, he found Chet crouching on the floor just back of the door. He yawned as Clay entered the apartment.

"What are you doing here?" asked Clay, in amazement.

"Guess I'm trying to find my way to the door!" was the half-smiling reply. "I didn't seem to know where I was when I woke up!"

Clay accepted the excuse, and went on with his preparation of breakfast. However, he doubted what the boy had said. Notwithstanding the previous good impression he had formed of the waif, he wondered if the lad had not crept out of bed and stationed himself by the door in order to hear what was said about the disposition of the gems.

"I'll have to be more careful," Clay thought. "That boy is a clever one!"

After breakfast the waif was rigged out with a suit of Alex.'s clothes. In the new attire he seemed to be a different boy from the one taken from the camp.

The boys did not accept as the truth all he said about himself, though that was not much. When he declared that he had never had any home, they commented on the fact that his speech and manners were those of a boy who had been given a fair education.

Chet at once took to the pets of the boat, Mose, Captain Joe, and Teddy, the bear cub, and they immediately recognized him as a member of the family.

While he was playing with the cub on the prow, Clay made an oblong package of the diamonds, scattering them in between sheets of paper, and marked them "Bonds." The bag in which they had been found was half filled with burrs, and small bits of a broken dish and tied tight. It resembled the bag as it had stood before any change had been made when Clay had finished with it.

This bag Clay resolved to keep in his pocket until he could place it under the eyes of the boy who claimed it, the idea being to see if he really would snatch the supposed prize and take to the river again. Clay hoped that he would not, for all liked the little fellow. That afternoon they ran down to a Memphis pier and Clay went ashore with the gems.

He was in time to secure a deposit box at a bank and stow the diamonds away. The cashier with whom he did business asked questions regarding his age and permanent residence, and seemed satisfied with his answers. He was, indeed, especially interested in Clay's description of the Rambler and the voyages the boys had made in her, and asked permission to visit the party that evening if he found time.

Clay gladly gave the required permission, ordered supplies sent to the pier, and then started out for a look at the beautiful city. Almost at the entrance to the bank he met Alex., who had the flushed appearance of a boy who had been walking pretty fast.

The two walked together for a block without speaking, save for the initial greeting, and then Alex. proposed that they go to a restaurant and have a "steak about as big as a parlor rug," as he expressed it. Clay agreed, but laughed at the notion.

"Why not take it on board?" he asked. "We can cook it much better than any city chef," he added.

"Well," Alex. replied, "I saw a neat little restaurant back here, not far from the river front, and I thought I'd like to go there and have a feed."

So the two turned into the restaurant, when they came to it, and took a small table at a rear corner of the room. It being late for dinner and early for supper, there were few in the place.

One party, at the front of the room, at once attracted Clay's attention. There were three men in the party, one young, smiling and flashily dressed; one old, grizzled and clad in a well-worn business suit; and another dressed expensively and with great care. This man had a surprising growth of red hair which showed evidences of great care. His face was smooth-shaven, and had the appearance of having recently been divested of a beard, the flesh showing soft and white, as if not long exposed to the weather.

When this man arose to pay the check and laid a hand on the back of a chair, Clay noticed that the hand was very large and finely kept. The man was something over six feet in height! Clay gave Alex. a kick under the table and directed his gaze to the large man, then passing over to the cashier's window.

"Take a good look at that man," he whispered. "Ever see him before?"

"I saw him when I passed," was the reply, "and brought you here. That's Red, the Robber."

CHAPTER XIV – ALEX. BREAKS FURNITURE

"Unless Red, the Robber, has a twin who is an exact duplicate of himself," Clay whispered, "that is just who it is!"

"When I passed here," Alex. explained, "the three were just sitting down to dinner, and I knew that I could get you back here in time to see Red, the Robber, before he could finish the big steak he had just tackled. There he is! Now what?"

"It doesn't seem possible that that finely-dressed, well-groomed man is really the one who talked with us out on the river at Cairo, and who afterwards captured the Rambler by holding a gun about the size of a cannon on me," Clay declared.

"And the man who bespoke kind treatment for Chet, the waif," Alex. went on. "I guess we're both seeing things not present to the senses! There ain't no such man!"

"It can't be!" Clay tried to convince himself. "It can't be the same man!"

Yet he knew deep down in his heart that it was the same man! If there had been any doubt of the complete identification at the start, there was none when the man spoke to the cashier in the full, deep voice which Clay knew that he had heard while he was tied up in the cabin of the Rambler!

"I have heard that river thieves sometimes make up to look like bankers and high-up politicians," Alex. whispered.

"And I have heard that bankers and high-up politicians occasionally assume the disguises of river characters for some purpose of their own," Clay returned.

"Do they mix with murderers and steal motor boats when they do that?" asked Alex., with a provoking snicker. "'Cause if they do, this may be one of the high-ups!"

"He must recognize us," Clay went on. "Watch and see if you catch in him any signs of joy at the meeting!"

"He hasn't yet shown that he knows we are in the room," Alex. replied.

"There's one way to find out who he is," Clay suggested. "When he leaves here, you follow him until he enters some house or office and ask questions about him after he goes on. I'll do the same here—that is, I'll see what the cashier knows about him."

Alex., glad of an opportunity of showing what he could accomplish as a detective, readily agreed to this arrangement, and, the man leaving the restaurant at the moment, Alex. darted away after him, leaving Clay to question the cashier.

The big man, still in the company of his two companions, walked briskly toward the river front, after leaving the restaurant, and finally came to a stop at a pier some distance down the stream from that at which the motor boat lay. Alex. watched the three men shake hands gravely and part, the one he believed to be Red going on board a small steamer which lay close by with smoke pouring from her stacks.

"Now," thought the boy, "shall I give it up, or shall I sneak on board the boat and see what I can learn of this man who poses as a river pirate one day and as a gentleman of great respectability the next?"

Alex.'s horse sense told him to wait about the pier until some one came off the boat and engage that person in conversation in an effort to learn the identity of the man he was following, but his natural love of adventure told him to make his way on board and learn there what he could, not only of the man, but of the steamer and its destination and cargo.

The spirit of adventure won, and Alex., waiting until there was no one in sight on the freight deck, ventured on board. There was still no one in sight when he reached the staircase leading to the cabin, and he proceeded to climb up, listening between steps for indications of human life.

He found the indications he sought with a vengeance at the head of the stairs. As he stepped up a husky negro seized him by the collar and dragged him toward the prow. Alex. kicked and struggled to no purpose. The negro was too strong for him. All the time he was carrying him along, almost as he would have carried a kitten, the negro kept up a running fire of comment.

The boy gathered from this comment that he was regarded as a sneak thief, and tried more than once to explain, but the negro kept on talking to himself and paid no attention to the words of his prisoner. Alex. administered a sturdy kick and gave it up.

Presently a door was opened at the very front end of the cabin and the boy was thrust into a small stateroom. The force of his entrance sent him against a berth and he crawled up and lay down to think things over. He heard the door behind him locked.

"This is a pretty kettle of fish!" grunted the boy, as he looked about the room.

It was just an ordinary stateroom, with one bunk, a dresser, and a chair. The window looking out on deck was covered by green slat-blinds, and ornamental metal-work covered the glass panel of the door opening into the cabin.

After taking in the room in all its details, Alex. arose and tried to open the green blinds so as to get a look outside. To his surprise he found that they would not open. They were of steel, and were there to protect the window! The room was as stoutly guarded as a prison cell!

"Red, the Robber, seems to have use for a cell," the boy thought, "that is, if this is his boat! I wonder what he thinks he's going to do with me?"

Alex. had now no doubt that Red had recognized Clay and himself at the restaurant. He wondered if Clay, too, had been trapped! He could not make up his mind as to whether the man was a robber or a gentleman of business standing, but he knew that he was in a most undesirable situation.

Then he began to wonder if Red knew that he was on board! The man had given no intimation that he had knowledge of being followed. He, Alex., had sneaked on board, like a veritable wharf rat, and the husky negro had been fully justified in taking him into custody! Still, the negro should have listened to his explanations and given him a chance to prove his innocence.

This last view of the case was much more to the liking of the boy than the previous one, for Red had shown a friendly spirit while on board the Rambler, and might now set him free as soon as informed of his capture. Clay had permitted Red his freedom under much more trying conditions!

"If he's a river thief," Alex. concluded, "he'll keep me here until he is sure I can't injure him by telling of his raid on the motor boat, but if he is on the level—if he was, for some purpose of his own, masquerading while in company with Sam—he will release me as soon as he knows I am here—for Clay's sake, if not for my own!"

This was a rather comforting conclusion, so the boy began beating with all his might on the panels of the door. He pounded away for some moments without hearing the least response, and then sat down to rest.

While he sat there on the berth, panting from his unnoticed exertions, the boat quivered in all its timbers, the noise of escaping steam reached his ears, and then he knew that the steamer was under way. This was the worst thing that could happen to the boy, and he knew it.

The steamer might go to Cuba, or to the upper reaches of the Missouri or the Mississippi, separating him from his chums for weeks. If Red really was a robber, he would not take the chance of releasing him, for that would give him an opportunity to warn those on board the Rambler, as well as to report to the police the illegal seizure of the motor boat!

"I'm going to find out about this!" Alex. declared, springing off the berth. "I'm going to do an English suffragette stunt and smash windows!"

As his whole mind was set on making a noise so as to attract the attention of the man he had followed on board, the boy was by no means conservative in his next move.

First he took the light-framed chair which stood by the berth and smashed it against the fancy metal work which protected the glass panel. The chair went to pieces without touching the glass, so Alex. took up a slender leg and, poking it through in between the metal work, punched out the pane.

It fell back into the cabin with a rattle, and then Alex., putting his face close to the opening, let out a yell which would have done credit to an Apache Indian on the warpath! In the meantime the steamer was backing out into the current.

"I guess that will let 'em know they have a cabin passenger!" Alex. grunted, as he began tossing the fragments of the chair out on the cabin floor.

The boy was just considering the firing of his automatic, which had not been taken from him by the negro, when a heavy voice near at hand broke into a hearty laugh, and the face of the red-headed man appeared before the opening, half-shielded by an arm, for the boy was still looking for things to throw through.

"What seems to be the difficulty?" the man asked, and Alex. thought he saw a twinkle of humor in the blue eyes fixed upon him.

"No difficulty at all," Alex. answered, with a touch of irony in his tone. "I'm just doing this for exercise, and to make business for boat builders!"

"Of course," laughed the man, "you wouldn't come out if I should unlock the door?"

"Oh, I don't know," Alex. replied. "I've got a good deal of work to do in here yet, and I might bring back an axe to help out."

"You'll find that the berth is of steel," the red-headed man said. "You can't chop that up. How long will it take you to finish the dresser? I might come back and let you out as soon as you have got through with that!"

"All right!" grinned the boy, "anything to oblige," and he went at the dresser with the leg of a chair!

The giant unlocked the door, stepped inside, and, taking Alex. by the ear, marched him out of the wrecked room. Once in the cabin he let go of the ear and walked toward the stern with a hand on the boy's arm.

"You wasn't so giddy the last time I saw you!" declared the boy.

The man laughed, opened the door of a large stateroom toward the stern, pushed the boy inside, and stepped in after him. This was a handsome room, elaborately furnished. Alex. dropped into a chair and looked about.

The steamer now seemed to be making fast time down the river, and Alex. looked out of a window in the hope of seeing the location of the Rambler.

"Say," he finally asked, wrinkling his freckled nose at the man, "what is the answer to this? I give it up!"

"What was it you boys put in the deposit box at the bank?" asked the man.

"I didn't put anything in; I didn't go to any bank."

"But your chum did. You met him at the bank entrance, and brought him back to look at me! You know what he put in the vault box. What was it?"

"It was a long package marked bonds," was the boy's reply.

"But did the package contain bonds?"

"I don't know; I never saw the inside of it," answered Alex., wondering if this man had followed all their movements since being allowed to leave the Rambler.

"Perhaps the lad you call Clay will tell," smiled the giant. "Or the boys on the Rambler may give the information I seek—when you both fail to return to-night."

"So you've got Clay, too, have you?" shouted Alex., and he make a rush for the door!

CHAPTER XV — THE LEATHER BAG MISSING

When Clay went to the cashier's desk to pay the check for the meals the two boys had eaten, also with a view of finding out what was known there of the red-headed man, he asked the first question which came into his mind.

"Is that the sheriff—the tall man with the red hair?"

The cashier eyed the boy keenly for a moment and then answered the question by asking one, as many who wait on the public have a habit of doing.

"Why? Do you want to see the sheriff?" he asked, suspiciously.

Clay was provoked, but tried not to show it as he replied,

"I thought I knew the man, that's all. Perhaps I was mistaken, for he would have recognized me, I'm certain, if he had ever seen me before."

"Well, that's not the sheriff," the cashier replied, more civilly; "I don't know who he is. He came in here this forenoon, for the first time, with those two men, and he has been in here twice since. There are others with him, too, for people kept coming in and making reports of some kind to him. One made a sign to him, through the glass, while you were eating. He may be a crook, for all I know."

Clay thanked the cashier and went away, turning in the direction of the river front immediately. At the next corner he came face to face with the cashier of the bank where he had secured the deposit box. The banker extended a hand in greeting.

"I was just wishing," he said, "that I could run across you this afternoon. I have a little spare time, and I'd like to look over that wonderful boat of yours. Not long ago I saw a full-page description of your river trips in a Chicago newspaper."

"Come along, then," Clay replied. "You'll have a good chance to see it by daylight if you go now. It isn't very much of a boat, but we're proud of it. It is just an ordinary motor boat, with electrical attachments which provide for lighting and cooking. There's also a little refrigerator, cooled by water, and a container for holding electricity in storage, so we have plenty of light when the boat is not running. But come along and take a look at it."

As the two walked arm-in-arm down the street two men fell in behind them, moving as they moved, fast or slow, and stopping whenever the cashier drew up to explain some city feature to the boy. After a couple of blocks of this work, the two walked faster and, coming in advance of the two they had followed, turned about and greeted the cashier warmly. They were promptly introduced to Clay as Hilton and Carney.

"We're just going to the river to look over the Rambler, the famous motor boat we have talked so much about," Benson, the cashier said. "If Mr. Emmett, here, has no objections, I'd like to have you go along with us."

"No objections whatever," Clay responded. "There isn't much to see, but such as it is you are welcome to have a look."

Clay did not observe the significant look which passed from the cashier to the two men, as they walked along toward the boat. They soon reached the pier and went aboard theRambler, finding Case, Chet, Jule and Mose there. The bear cub attracted a great deal of attention, and Chet seemed to take special interest in the doings of the party.

The three men did not hurry themselves at all, but took their time about everything. They inspected the bunks and the cupboard, and even looked into the storage places under the decks and the cabin floor.

Clay was with them most of the time, but now and then they halted and conversed together in low tones, so, of course, the boy dropped away from the group. He considered this a strange proceeding on the part of the guests, but said nothing.

Finally they asked Clay all sorts of questions about their progress down the river, when they left Rock Island, when they touched at St. Louis, and when they reached Cairo. The boy, though wondering, answered the rather personal questions frankly.

It was almost dark when the visitors left the boat. Their last visit had been made to the cabin, to inspect the electric stove, and they passed the boys on the prow as they went ashore. For a time after their departure the boys discussed the unusual conduct of the visitors, and then Chet and Clay went in to prepare supper.

Taking advantage of a momentary absence of Chet from the cabin, Clay looked in the hiding-place where he had left the leather bag in which the diamonds had been brought on shore. The bag was gone! Clay hastened out on deck to meet two astonished boys.

"Say," Case said, "what's come over Chet? He came out of the cabin like a shot and jumped off on the pier. Then, without even stopping to look back, he ran down into the city! What have you been doing to him?"

Clay stood for a moment like one incapable of speech, then he dropped into a deck-chair and laughed until the tears ran down his cheeks. Captain Joe and Teddy joined the others in their criticism of his strange actions.

"You didn't get too many high balls while in the city, did you?" asked Case.

"You might have kept sober enough to bring Alex. back with you!" Jule put in.

"Ah believe yo' done scare dat lad off de boat!" little Mose suggested.

"Well," Clay explained, presently, "I suppose I ought to treat the matter more seriously, for we may have lost Chet for good, but it is funny for all that."

"Why don't you pass it around?" demanded Case. "Let us in on the laugh!"

"You all know what I did with the articles we found on Chet," Clay responded. "Well, when I took the valuables out of the leather bag, I put burrs from the repair kit and pieces of broken dishes into the bag and hid it where I thought Chet might find it if he looked long enough."

"I don't see anything funny in that," observed Case, with a frown.

"Just wait! When I looked for the bag, just now, it was gone, and the next thing I hear is that Chet has taken to his heels. You see what has happened!"

"The poor little chap!" exclaimed Case. "I'm sorry for him."

"So am I," Clay agreed, "but he ought to have been honest with us."

"We knew what to expect," Jule suggested. "He said he'd get the gems back if he could, didn't he? Now he thinks he's got them, and is lugging off a lot of truck not worth a cent! I call that a shame!"

Clay looked thoughtful for a second and then burst out:

"But is he? Look here, fellows," he went on, excitedly, "suppose he never took the bag at all! Suppose Chet found it and changed his mind about running off with it! Suppose one of the visitors took it! Suppose that is what they were here for; suppose Chet missed it as soon as they went away and chased on after them!"

"You said the visitors were bankers!" exploded Jule. "What about that?"

"One of them was, but I don't know anything about the others. Strange they should all be so eager to inspect the Rambler! Strange they should get off by themselves and talk in whispers! I reckon we're knee-deep in mystery!"

"Well, where did you leave Alex.?" asked Jule. "He hasn't come back yet!"

"And here's another funny thing," Clay went on, without answering the question, directly. "We saw Red, the Robber, up town, dressed like a gentleman! Alex. followed him out of the place where we saw him, and may have got into trouble!"

"Then the stealing of the bag is Red's work!" decided Case. "No need to guess about that any more! How he got his men in with the banker I don't know, but he did it, and one of them took it, and poor Chet saw that it was gone, and now he is following a bag filled with crockery about the city!"

"Pshaw!" Jule exclaimed. "It is dollars to doughnuts that Chet got the bag himself! He said he'd swipe it if he got a chance. You all know that!"

A figure now came dashing down the pier at break-neck speed and Alex. leaped on the deck and dropped into a chair, wiping the sweat from his face.

"Did you find who he was?" asked Clay, as the boys all gathered around Alex.

Alex. told the story of the steamer and the wrecked stateroom, and ended with the talk he had had with Red, while the boys looked on in wonder at the odd twist things were getting into. Even Teddy Bear seemed impressed by the mystery, Jule declared!

"And how did you get away from him?" demanded Case. "How did you get back here?"

"I jumped and ran, and he caught me," was the reply. "Then he made me promise not to say a word about his escapade on the Rambler and let me go! Can you beat it?"

"What did he have you locked up for?" asked Clay. "I don't understand that."

"Just because he wanted that promise," Alex. suggested. "Is that the answer?"

"It may be," Clay admitted, "but here's the question: Is he a robber or a detective? Is he on the level, or is he just a clever scoundrel?"

"Perhaps Alex. can judge better of that when he knows what has taken place here," Case suggested, going on with the story of the disappearance of the leather bag.

"Red's gang got it," laughed Alex., without a moment's hesitation, as Case finished the story. "He knew Clay put something in the bank, and asked me what it was. Yes, we know all about it now!"

"I just believe Chet took the bag, thinking the gems were in it," insisted Jule.

"We'll never know the truth until we find the lad," Clay said, with a sigh.

"Unless Red, the Robber, shows up again in a confidential mood," Alex. laughed.

"If the supplies I ordered are all in," Clay went on, "I think we'd better be on our way. There's mystery in the very air here!"

"If we stay here long," Alex. prophesied, "the coon I biffed on the shin may show up, lookin' for revenge, or Red may come after pay for the furniture I smashed!"

"What did he say about that furniture?" grinned Jule. "You've got the nerve!"

"He never mentioned it," was the reply. "Say," the lad went on, "I believe that chap is all to the good, after all! He seemed to think the smash act was funny."

During the afternoon Case and Mose had caught a large fish and Chet had succeeded in bringing down a wild duck, so the cooking of supper was an elaborate affair. Then Clay made light biscuits and coffee, and fried potatoes, and the boys were as happy as well-fed boys with no one to "boss," usually are, except that they missed Chet.

After supper they discussed the proposition of waiting there a day in the hope of finding the runaway boy, but it was finally decided that he could find them easier than they could find him, so they started the motors and went on toward the Gulf.

The early part of the night was bright, so the boys ran down about twenty miles, as the river ran, and then tied up below a "tow-head" which stuck up out of the water below an island of good size. They found it necessary to take this precaution always, for the wash of large steamers passing up and down would have rattled things in the Rambler, if the motor boat was not capsized.

At midnight the sky became overcast with threatening clouds and the wind blew in fitful gusts. There seemed to be no danger of their being disturbed by visitors that night, but all the same they thought best to station a watchman, and Case volunteered to keep awake and see that "no one flew away with the boat," as he expressed it.

Somewhere about two o'clock in the morning, the boy, who was having hard work keeping awake, heard the puff and bellow of an approaching steamer, toiling up against the strong current. Almost at the same instant he felt a jar, as if the boat had been struck by floating driftwood. He switched on the prow light to see what was doing, but quickly extinguished it as the steamer came up and a heavy rowboat dropped away from her!

CHAPTER XVI—WHAT DROPPED ON DECK

"I guess my turning on that light started something!" the boy mused, as he darkened the small electric globe in the cabin and sat down to await developments. He kept just inside the cabin door at first, for the wind was cold and searching.

For a few moments he could hear the working of oars and the push of the current on an advancing boat, and then all was silent save the sighing of the wind and the wash of the river, still burdened at times with floating wreckage. It seemed to him that the boat which had slipped away from the steamer had anchored somewhere near the Rambler.

"I fully believe," Case grunted, as he finally left the cabin and looked out upon the dim river from the deck, "that if we should fly through the air on a cloud there would be some scamp watching us from another cloud! It's rotten, the way we are chased about!"

The boy did not know that his complaint had found words until he heard a chuckle close to his side and turned about to faintly distinguish the freckled face of Alex., who stood looking over the river to the south.

"You've got no kick coming!" Alex. declared. "You wouldn't go on these river trips if we found nothing more than scenery, any more than I would! It seems like living to be chased about, as you call it! If it wasn't for the mystery and adventure in the jaunts I'd be at home in little old Chicago—and that's where you'd be, too!"

"Well," Case returned, "I'd like to get one night off occasionally!"

"What is it now?" asked Alex. "I heard the steamer pass, but that didn't mean anything to me. What's going wrong now? Tell your old uncle Alex. all about it!"

"Uncle nothing!" laughed Case, restored to better humor by the optimism of the other. "If you want to know what's on the string, go and get a glass and try to find a rowboat in this mess of river and black sky. A safety razor that won't cut air will be given to the first one that discovers the boat!"

"Oh!" cried Alex. "There's a boat watching us! All right! Now I feel better! I was beginning to wonder when we'd have something to stir us up!"

"The boat dropped off when the steamer went up," Case explained. "I saw it under the lights, but of course it vanished in the darkness as soon as the big boat passed."

"There's something going on, then!" Alex. declared. "Of course they wouldn't know on board the steamer in the dark, that we were here, and so the thing which is going to happen is set to come off on shore. I'm going to stay awake and see what it is."

"You see," Case stated, hesitatingly, "I heard a bump on the hull of the Rambler, just as the steamer was churning into sight, around that bend, and turned on the prow light to see about it! That's why the rowboat dropped off here, I take it."

Alex. gave vent to a long, low whistle.

"Then we've got into the spot-light again!" he said. "It won't be any trouble for me to keep awake now! Shall we tell Clay the glad news, or let him sleep?"

"Oh, let him sleep! We can run this watch, all right!"

While the boys whispered and listened, the long, bellowing roar of a locomotive whistle came to their ears from the east. Then came the distant rumble of a train.

"What do you make of that?" asked Case. "I thought we were in the heart of a wild river country, and here come a train of cars – palace cars, I'll go you, at that!"

"About three or four miles from the river, in the state of Mississippi," laughed Alex., "runs the old Yazoo & Mississippi railroad. There are little towns all along its line. Perhaps the boat dropped off the steamer to make one of the country bergs! We never thought of that, did we?"

Case pulled the other by the arm and both drew away from the gunwale.

"There's a boat out there now," he declared, in a whisper. "I heard the tunk of an oar then! I'll bet they are trying to get on board!"

"Got your gun?" asked Alex.

"Sure thing I have," was the reply.

"And your searchlight?"

"You know it!"

"So have I," Alex. went on. "Now, if they try to board the Rambler, we'll lie low until they begin to climb over the rail. Then we'll turn on our electrics. If they are strangers, and look like river pirates, we'll shoot them up! What?"

"But why not turn on the prow light?" asked Case.

"Because we can handle the electric flashlights quicker. If we have to show the light and shoot, be quick to change your position after the light is switched off. Then, if they shoot back, they won't hit you."

There was a boat approaching. There was no doubt about that. And the people on board of her were doing their best to keep their movements from being known by those of theRambler. Case and Alex. could hear the dash of oars, and now and then a rough command. The two boys sat in silence and waited.

Then, as Case and Alex. afterward complained, something happened which "spoilt all the fun!" Captain Joe came out of the cabin and gave forth a series of threatening growls, and Teddy added to the warning by saying things in bear talk!

The mysterious boat came on no longer. There were still sounds of the working of a heavy craft in a strong current, but these gradually died out.

"I'd like to throw you both into the river after them!" Alex. scolded at the animals, as they came around him, asking to be congratulated on their success in driving off the visitors! "Now we'll be haunted by those fellows for a week, while if you had kept quiet we'd have settled with them right here!"

"Suppose we turn on the power and chase 'em up?" asked Case.

"And give them a chance to do all the shooting!" replied Alex. scornfully. "I'm not looking for a watery grave in the Mississippi."

"Well," Case continued, "if you don't want to follow them up, just to see what they look like, perhaps we'd better drop down a short distance. If we can't fight them, we don't want to feel that they're right under our noses, waiting for a chance to get us into a hole! I'd rather face a hundred men in the open than know that one was skulking about me in the darkness!"

"This is a fierce old stream for strangers to travel on in the dark!" Alex. said.

"I know it, but— —"

Before the boy could finish the sentence a faint jar came, as if some person had caught hold of the anchor chain and given it a pull, or hung his weight on it.

"There's our friend!" Case whispered. "Now, get ready with your gun!"

In a second, while the boys listened, they heard a hard substance fall on the deck. Alex.'s light flashed around the gunwale, but there was no one in sight.

In the middle of the deck, however, still dripping from the river, lay the leather bag which had held the diamonds, and which had held only burrs and broken crockery when last seen on board the Rambler! Alex. picked it up, found that it was still half full of some hard substances, and shut off the light.

"You saw it?" he asked of Case, as he cuddled down by the boy's side.

"Of course! The leather bag!"

"What do you think of it?" demanded Alex.

"I don't think!" admitted Case. "I've lost the power of thought!"

"But what did they throw it back here for?" insisted Alex.

"Why did who throw it back here?" chuckled Case.

"Now, look here, Smarty," Alex. continued. "There are only four persons who could have taken that bag from the boat, the cashier and his two friends, and Chet."

"Unless the dog ate it, or Teddy threw it overboard."

"Oh, quit your foolishness! Now, which one of the four is out there in the river? Whoever it is has a sense of humor, for the tossing of the bag back shows that the situation is appreciated."

"You notice the steamer came UP the river?" asked Case.

"Yes; what of it?" demanded Alex. "I don't see anything in that."

"Well, that shows that whoever threw the bag on deck came from down stream! It shows, too, that we have been watched every minute, for reasons which we don't know anything about!"

"Yes, in order to keep track of us they might have taken the railroad down the river bank and then taken a steamer up, so as to meet us on the way down! I see something in it now. But who is it?"

"It may be Chet!" suggested Case. "He may have returned the bag just to show us that he knows about the removal of the diamonds."

"I just believe Chet is out there somewhere, and that he would come on board if he knew we wouldn't raise a row about the way he left us!" declared Alex.

"I give it all up!" Case returned. "It's your watch now, and I'm going to bed! If there's anything good to eat thrown on deck out of the darkness, just wake me up, otherwise let me alone. I'll hunt up my dream book to-morrow and find what it says about leather bags dropping out of the sky!"

Alex. sat alone in the dim night, watching the river and the dark bottom lands of the island for a long time before anything attracted his attention. Then a light, like that made by a camp-fire, sprang up on the Mississippi side of the river.

He could see figures moving about in front of the blaze, but of course could not distinguish faces. Presently the low, weird chant of a plantation song came over the waters. It was evident that a gang of negroes, possibly railroad repair men, was passing the night in camp on the shore.

As Alex. listened to the plaintive songs he heard a splash in the water at the side of the boat, and shot his light in that direction. A stick was floating away, and the boy concluded that it was that which had made the noise he had heard.

He heard the negroes come to the bank of the river to gather driftwood for the fire, and heard their drawling voices saying something of the river going down fast, but could not catch the full import of their words.

The companionship of the fire and the voices was something to the boy, and he sat until daylight began to show in perfect contentment. Then he went into the cabin to get a line, it being his idea to surprise the boys with a fish breakfast.

He looked at the sleeping faces for a moment and started when he came to a rug in the corner where Mose usually slept! Captain Joe was there, his nose in his paws, but Mose was not there! Alex. searched the boat. The negro boy was gone! The amazed boy half pulled Clay out of his bunk and began the story of the night.

"We're not yet out of the enchanted land," he said. "We are still seeing things! The leather bag comes back out of the sky, and Mose goes up in the air. I'm for getting down to the Gulf right soon."

"Have you looked in the bag for any solution of the puzzle?" asked Clay. "There may be a note of some kind there: a note of explanation. See?"

"Yes," declared Alex., pointing over the side, and not answering the question about the bag, "I see that we are stuck in the mud, and not likely to get out until another flood, a year, or perhaps two years, off."

CHAPTER XVII – GETTING OUT OF THE MUD

Clay's face plainly expressed the dismay he felt as he bent over the gunwale and looked downward in the growing light of the morning. The Rambler lay in a bed of soft, oozy mud, with harder ground between her and the "tow-head."

"I presume," Alex. said, "that the people of this country will be glad to see that the river lowered in the night! So are we?"

"We ought to have provided against this," Clay exclaimed, in self-reproach. "We might just as well have anchored a few yards farther down. What next, I wonder?"

"The longer we wait before getting the motor boat into the water," Alex. said, "the harder work it will be, for the river is lowering every minute."

Clay scratched his head and estimated the distance to deep water.

"We'll have to put on our bathing suits and take to the mud," he decided. "By all taking hold, we may be able to get her out of this mess. Nice job it is, too!"

"Sure!" Alex. grinned. "Mud baths are healthful! There's Mike Cogan, the Chicago politician, he goes to take mud baths twice a year! If we had him here now we wouldn't charge him a cent for his cure! I think he'd like it, too."

"I'll wake Case and Jule, and we'll get right at it," Clay said. "I wish a lot of husky plantation hands would happen along in a shanty boat."

"There was a group of them over on the Mississippi side last night," Alex. explained. "We might get them, if they are there yet. Say," he continued, with a grin, "I believe that is where the little coon went! He saw the camp-fire and heard the plantation songs, and couldn't remain away from his own people!"

"In that case," Clay suggested, "the little rascal will be back soon."

"Never can tell about boys of the Mose stripe," Alex. predicted. "He may follow the men off and never show up here again."

Clay started for the cabin to arouse Case and Jule and then turned back to ask:

"Did that pocket book—the bag, rather, that had the diamonds in, make its appearance before or after Mose disappeared?"

"I don't know when Mose lit out," was the reply. "At one time I heard a splash in the river and looked to see what it was about, but Mose was not in sight then. There was only a large stick floating in the stream. Still, he might have gone at that time. If he did, he left long after the bag was thrown on deck. What about it?"

"I was thinking that he might have followed off the person who threw the bag," Clay explained, "though I can't understand why he should have gone away so secretly. Did the dog make any remarks about the time the bag reached the deck?"

"Nix on Captain Joe! He's getting too sleepy! He stirred only once in the night, and that was when the boat was coming up to us. He frightened the pirates away, when Case and I had planned to shoot 'em up!"

"Then," concluded Clay, "when we reach the truth of it, we'll discover that it was Chet who was around here last night, and who threw the bag on deck. You know we have been thinking, all along, that he might have taken it."

"That's what Jule insists on," Alex. returned, "while the rest of us think one of the visitors took it, and that Chet chased off the boat to get it back, not knowing that the diamonds had been taken out of it."

"It seems clear now," Clay replied, "that Chet took it. In the first place, there is no good reason for supposing that the visitors would find the bag, or take it if they did find it; or take any trouble to return it after they had found its contents of no value. Chet got it, all right, and, disappointed and chagrined at the substitution we had made, he lost no time in throwing it back at us."

"Chet was broke, wasn't he?" asked Alex., with a sly grin.

"So far as I know, yes. Anyway, he didn't look like a millionaire when we took him on board and fixed him out with a suit of your clothes!"

"Then how would he ride up the river in a steamer, or ride down the river to the next town to take the steamer, or hire a rowboat and pay the captain of the steamer for letting him off in his boat as soon as he saw the light of the Rambler?"

"You smash all my solutions," laughed Clay. "Now, give me one of your own, so I can smash that,"

"I ain't no prophet!" grinned the red-headed boy, "but I'm gambling that when we get down to the bottom of matters we'll find Red, the Robber, in the mess!"

"We have already found him in the mess," laughed Clay. "He knew, according to your story, that I had put something in the safety vaults! Besides, he seemed to own the steamer you were on, didn't he?"

"He seemed to be the boss."

"Suppose we quit guessing and get the Rambler out of the mud," suggested Clay, then.

Case and Jule were called out on deck, and the lads, clad only in their bathing suits, were soon wallowing in the soft mud, which was so deep that they could get no footing at all, and so could not lift on the boat. In fact, the more they tried to lift the boat, to slide it toward deep water, the deeper she seemed to sink.

"We're up against a beautiful proposition!" Jule exclaimed, climbing back on deck and leaning over the gunwale. "If we jar the boat any more, we'll have to take a trip to China and pull it through from the other side!"

Clay plowed out of the mud and made his way to the "tow-head" where he began examining the growth of willows. He seemed satisfied with what he saw, for he began cutting the long wands and called to the others to join him.

"What's doing?" asked Case.

"This ain't no island improvement corporation!" Alex. grinned.

"I know what he's up to!" Jule shouted, and in a second he was off the deck, cutting willows and throwing them into a heap at the edge of the hard ground.

"We've got to make mattresses of these willows," Jule declared, wiping the sweat from his face. "I read about that in a paper not long ago."

"To sleep on?" asked Alex., with a wink at Case.

"Silly!" roared Jule. "Get busy, both of you."

When a great stack of the willow wands had been cut, Clay and Jule began roughly braiding them together. In this way two mattresses a foot in thickness and nearly twelve feet square were constructed before noon. During all this time the boys had seen nothing of Chet, of Mose, or of the negroes who had camped on the shore the previous night. They had also overlooked breakfast!

The novelty of their employment had so engaged their attention that they felt no need of food until Teddy appeared on the deck sitting up like a man, begging for his breakfast! Then Alex. threw down the wands he was carrying to Clay, who was doing the weaving at that time, and sprang over to the boat with a chuckle of amusement.

"You're all right, Teddy Bear!" he cried. "We don't know enough to eat when we're hungry, do we? We'll show 'em what it is to feed up right without delay."

"What you going to get for dinner?" demanded Jule, putting a hand to his stomach to show how empty it was. "I want a whale fried whole!"

"Get your whale, then," advised Alex.

"Perhaps you think I can't!" laughed Jule. "Pass out my line and rod and I'll show you whether I'm a fisherman or not!"

Alex. did as requested and Jule waded through the mud to where there was a bit of hard ground, next the island, with a little swirl of water close by.

"Watch me now!" he cried.

But the boys did not care to watch him. Case and Clay continued the work of braiding mattresses, and Alex. got out a gun and sat on deck watching for ducks, of which there were plenty in that vicinity. Presently a yell from Jule called the attention of the others to him. He was fighting a fish which seemed to the astonished boys to be not less than ten feet in length, and the fish was pulling him down stream.

"Give me a hand!" the boy shouted. "He's pulling me in!"

"Let go the line!" cried Alex.

"And lose it!" answered Jule. "Not much! Give me a hand!"

Case and Clay both rushed to the boy's assistance, and with great effort a monster fish was landed in the mud. Jule was jubilant.

"The biggest catch of the trip!" he declared. "Who says I can't produce a whale when I feel the need of a whole one fried?"

Case and Clay leaned back and screamed with amusement. Alex. looked on with a grin which was more provoking than the laughter of the others.

"Have all the fun you can," roared Jule, "but don't get gay!"

"Throw him back into the river!" Clay advised, poking at the catch. "That is just a big catfish, and no one eats them save the negroes! They're tougher than the tripe at Bill's restaurant, in Chicago!"

"I guess you won't throw him away!" yelled Jule.

"All right!" Clay answered. "Take him to bed with you, if you want to, but kindly see if you can't get a bass for our dinner. There are plenty of them in here."

Reluctantly Jule started the catfish back toward his natural element, and the big fellow seemed to thank him with a parting wave of his tail as he took to the water. In a few moments he had a fine large bass, weighing six or eight pounds, and before long Alex. had a couple of ducks, so work was suspended while dinner was cooked and eaten. After the meal the work was continued until Case declared there were enough willow mattresses on hand to float a city.

Then the mattresses were hauled alongside the Rambler and a considerable part of the cargo of the boat was put out on them. Thus lightened, and having a strong footing, the lads had no difficulty in pushing the Rambler out into deep water.

"What shall we do with the mattresses now?" asked Clay, as the boat swung off the bottom. "We have spent too much time on them to throw them away!"

"Tow them along," advised Case. "It won't cost us anything to tote them along, and we may have use for them. A man could build a tent on them, by fastening them together, and live there. I'm strong for taking them with us."

This was finally agreed to, and the boys were about to start down the stream again when a shout from the Mississippi side of the river attracted their attention.

"There's that little coon!" laughed Case. "See the rascal! He's going to swim to the boat, or going to try to!"

"He never can do it," Clay declared. "We'll have to swing the Rambler over that way and pick him up. He's making a swift run, though!"

"Well," Alex. replied, "just you look behind him and see what he's running from."

Half a dozen negroes and one white man were now seen running down the river bank in pursuit of Mose. They seemed to redouble their exertions when the Rambler shot over toward the boy, but were obliged to halt when the boy was picked up and the boat went on down stream, towing the willow mattresses in her wake!

Mose dropped down on deck, panting and rolling his eyes.

"Ah'm scared white!" he chattered. "Fo' de Lawd, dat's de man what trun dis coon an' Captain Joe into the ribber up no'th! Ah's scared of him!"

CHAPTER XVIII—SWEPT INTO A SWAMP

"Who threw you and Captain Joe into the river, up north?" demanded Jule. "Wake up and tell us what's the matter with you. What were those people chasing you for?"

Mose only sat up on deck and rolled his eyes as the Rambler increased the distance between the pursuers and himself. Seeing that he was now beyond their reach, he arose and leaned over the gunwale and made funny insulting faces at them.

"What does he mean?" asked Jule, turning to Clay. "Who's chasing him?"

"Don't you remember how Sam, the Robber, the fellow who, with Red, captured the Rambler in the bayou, threw the boy and the dog out, and how they lay in the grounds at the old house until dusk and then came to your rescue?" asked Clay. "You must have a poor memory, I think."

"I didn't know whether it was Red or Sam who threw him in," Jule explained.

"So that's Sam over there with the negroes?" questioned Alex. "What did you do to them, Mose? Where did you go last night? What do you mean by forming an exploring expedition all by yourself and having all the fun?"

"Ah went 'shore to hear de singin'," the boy replied, "an' dey cotch me stealin' de yaller leg chicken, an' say de's goin' to beat dis coon up plenty!"

"You swam all that way to steal a chicken?" asked Jule. "Was it cooked?"

"Yaller leg chicken!" insisted the boy.

"Was it cooked?" persisted Jule. "Where did they get it?"

"Dey say it done lef' de roos' an' follow dem into camp!"

"Did you eat a whole one?" asked Case. "A whole yellow-legged chicken?"

Mose grinned and showed the whites of his eyes.

"Ah shore did!" he replied, and Jule declared that he would willingly have helped him do it if he had only known about it!

"What were they talking about last night?" asked Clay, as the Rambler turned a bend and lost sight of the negroes and Sam, still gesticulating fiercely, on the east shore.

"They're sho' goin' to get you-all!" was the reply. "They goin' to steal dis boat, first thing you know. Ah'm scart ob dat white man!"

The little fellow could tell very little of the talk he had heard while detained in the negro camp. He knew that Sam, the Robber, was there with the negroes, and that he was continually urging them to help him secure the Rambler, but that was all. Of their plans he knew nothing but this.

During the afternoon the boys passed a great many steamers, going up the river, some with supplies for those who had been made homeless by the flood. Fortunately the levees had held, but the water had filled in back of them, in some instances and destroyed much property. The lagoons and swamps up river were still flooded, and in places farming land was still being washed away.

All the way down, until night closed in, they saw gangs of negroes on the levees, fishing drift wood out of the water. In some instances small out-houses were brought out in good condition. One shanty boat the boys saw had the cupola of a house set up on the prow, and a farm bell in the top of it was ringing as the raft bobbed in the currents of the river. Now and then families were seen gathered on the levees, evidently waiting for a steamer to take them off.

The boys kept up good speed until night and then tied up in a small cove on the lower side of an island, not far from the Mississippi side.

"We have been going pretty fast," Clay observed, as the boat was worked in behind a point so as to be out of the wash of the steamers. "We haven't a thing to do until we get back to Chicago, and we can take all the time we want getting back. How is that for a peaceful life, Mose?" he added, turning to the little negro boy.

Mose showed a mouthful of white teeth and a pair of chalk-white eyeballs.

"It takes a corkscrew to get conversation out of Mose!" Jule observed.

"I think I can make him talk," laughed Alex. "Mose," he went on, "I'll give you a plate of honey for supper if you'll tell me where Chet is and who threw the leather bag on deck last night?"

"Some one fro' what?" asked the little fellow.

"Some one threw this on the boat in the night," Alex. answered, handing the bag to the boy. "Did you hear any one around before you left?"

The negro boy rolled his eyes for a minute then took the bag and held it under the nose of Captain Joe, who sniffed at it for a second and then walked back to the place in the cabin where Chet had slept.

"De dawg sho' know who fro' dat bag!" he said, patting Captain Joe on the head.

"That shows why the dog didn't make a row when the person who threw it got close enough to the boat to heave it on deck!" Jule laughed.

"It takes a little coon to find out things about animals!" grinned Alex. "Here we've been studying over who tossed the bag, and Mose settles the question in a minute. That is sure some coon!"

"There's an affinity between a boy and a dog, anyway!" Clay laughed.

"I wonder if the kid is right?" Case questioned.

The boys discussed the matter during supper, and, right or wrong, Mose was given his plate of honey, which he was obliged to divide with Teddy!

The night passed away without incident, and early morning found the Rambler on her way to the Gulf again. The day was not different from other days for a week. The boys passed plantations and villages, swamps and lagoons, which seemed to have escaped the force of the flood, but now and then came to a wrecked cabin toppling from a bank.

They secured a supply of gasoline at a small place near the Arkansas line and at night found themselves in the heart of a desolate country. When they tied up they were at the mouth of a lagoon which seemed to lead into a great swamp.

"It is a sure thing that no leather bags will be thrown on deck to-night," Clay observed, as supper was prepared. "We are even off the track of the steamers, for they seem to stick to the opposite side of the stream."

"This would be a dandy spot for a band of river pirates to inhabit," Jule added.

"Don't talk about pirates!" admonished Clay. "You'll have Mose turning white again. Some day he'll turn so white with fright that he will never turn black again, and he wouldn't like that, would you, Mose?"

"Ah's 'tented wif mah color," answered the boy.

"That's all right, as long as you are on the boat," Alex. put in, "but you jump into the lagoon and see how long you'll last. An alligator will leave a fat pig any time to make a dinner off a black boy!"

"Quit scaring the boy!" exclaimed Case. "First thing you know, he will be afraid to swim ashore to steal a yellow-legged chicken roasted by tramps!"

When darkness fell a soft wind came out of the west and a slow rain began falling. It was wild and uncanny outside, but bright and warm in the cabin. Alex. entertained his chums for a time with stories of the Mississippi, and explained how Grant had shortened the stream by cutting a new channel at Vicksburg, but all were tired, and by nine o'clock all were asleep save Jule, who was to stand guard that night, and Mose who was moving restlessly about.

"Come on into the cabin, Mose," Jule finally ordered, "and go to bed, like a good coon! You'll get wet out on deck!"

The boy entered the cabin and sat down near the stove, in which a small fire was burning. Jule regarded him attentively.

"What's the matter with you to-night?" he finally asked.

"Ah hear a roar!" was the reply.

"That's the wind in the cypress trees," Jule explained.

"Is it de win' makes de ribber come up?" asked Mose, in a moment.

"Is the river rising?" asked Jule, going to the door and switching on the prow light. "It ought to be running down."

By the light of the electric the boy saw that the river was indeed rising. Little knolls which were above water when the boat had been anchored were now under a swift current. The river was sweeping past the mouth of the lagoon with a new force.

Presently trees and wreckage of different sorts were seen drifting down, and there came a rushing sound which added greatly to the weirdness of the scene.

"This beats me!" Jule muttered. "The flood has been going down for nearly a week. There must have been heavy rains up to the north, and at the sources of the rivers emptying into the Mississippi. I wonder if it will do anything to us?"

At that moment a timber crashed against the Rambler, jarring it considerably.

Clay and the others were out of their bunks in a minute, and out on deck to see what had taken place. Alex. was the first one to grasp the situation.

"We'll have to turn on the motors to hold this boat," he said. "The anchor lies in the mud, and will pull away at the first push of a current. First thing we know, we'll be down there in a cypress swamp!"

"You're excited!" Case called out. "We passed the flood two days ago."

"That's the trouble," Alex. explained. "We passed the flood! The crest of it is still to the north of us. It has undoubtedly been raining up river, and that has swelled the volume of water."

"Do you mean that we got down the river in advance of the flood?" demanded Case.

"We have been going a little faster than the current, haven't we, notwithstanding our tying up nights?" Alex. asked. "This little boat has been going some! To-night the crest of the flood overtakes us. See?"

"It doesn't look reasonable!" Case insisted. "I don't believe it!"

"The kid is right," Clay declared. "I have often read about boats meeting the flood the second time, once when they passed it, and once when it caught up with them."

The roaring sound which Mose had referred to now grew louder, sounding like the rush of a long and heavily loaded freight train.

While the lads listened, hardly knowing what to do to protect themselves, Mose pointed a shaking hand at a spot far down the lagoon. Clay looked and saw a great blaze on what seemed a wooded knoll to the west of the river.

"There's a camp down there!" he said.

"That makes it nice!" grinned Alex. "No honest men ever made camp in that hole at this season of the year! It is dollars to tripe that if we don't put on power the crest of the flood will wash us down, when the full strength comes, and beach us among a band of river pirates! If we don't get under way up stream we'll have do to something to make the anchor hold!"

While the boys were discussing some way of accomplishing this, for they did not like the idea of breasting the flood, the crest of the flood came seething down the stream, a wall of water four feet high! It swept over the point of land between the river and the bayou and dashed against the Rambler.

The anchor held for a minute, then the boys knew that they were in motion. The current seemed stronger there than in the river itself.

"The water is cutting a new channel below," Clay shouted, as the Rambler was swept away, "and we are headed for that swamp. Now, we are in a peck of trouble!"

CHAPTER XIX – PILGRIMS FROM OLD CHICAGO

The "peck of trouble" referred to as their portion by Clay turned out to be a full bushel, and good measure at that, in a very short time. Although the boys turned on the power – a thing they should have done long before – as soon as the crest of water came in sight, the Rambler was pitched down toward the swamp like a chip.

If the boys had been able to direct her course, they might have held her in the current, and so kept out of the muck hole into which she was swept when the water cut around a bend, driving straight on the shore. But just as the craft was getting under control a mass of limbs and canebrake tangled her propellers, and she went down with the flood, striking, as has been said, in a swamp where the head of the bayou had been, and into which the water still poured.

It was pitch dark out on the river and in the swamp, but the lights of the Rambler cast a circle of illumination about the spot where she lay, so that the black, bubbling water, with all the unclean reptiles it was forcing forth from their haunts, was in full view. It was carrying wreckage now, and this was piling up between the current and the boat, shutting off all chances of backing out, even if the current would have permitted it. It was indeed a desperate situation.

The motor boat had come to a stop against two monster cypress trees, between which she had wedged her nose. Only for this she might have been carried farther into the swamp, the water being deep for some distance ahead.

During the whirling passage down the bayou, while the boat was bumping against tree trunks and bounding off with a jar and a swish to go swinging around again, like a foolish dancer doing the time limit, Mose had clung tightly to one of Clay's legs. At the very beginning of that mad race he had caught sight of a couple of alligators, and was in deadly fear that they would climb on board and make a meal of him!

When the boat finally lodged between the giant trees, the little negro boy bounded from the deck and, seizing hold of a mass of vines, clambered up the tree to the west like a young monkey! Believing that he would have to help the others up, he carried a rope with him! Finally, sitting astride of a limb, he called down what he considered very good advice to the boys on the boat.

"Dey done get yo', sho'!" he warned. "Catch on de rope an' shin up!"

Serious as the situation was, with the water trinkling in over the stern of the motor boat, the boys grinned at each other at the fright of the boy.

"Come on down!" Alex. called. "If the boat should break away from the trees, you would be left alone in the swamp. Come on down and help get the boat out of this blessed swamp! You may get out with your rope and tow her if you want to!" he added, with a chuckle.

"Fo' de Lawd!" cried Mose, shuddering at the idea of getting into water inhabited by monsters who would leave a fat pig to feast off a black boy!

At least that was what one of the boys had said to him!

Attracted by the strange lights, walking and creeping things now began gathering in the shadows at the rim of the circle of light. Once Clay caught sight of the soft, appealing eyes of a deer, and now and then the howls of a swamp cat came to their ears above the roaring of the flood. Great water snakes struck their heads above the surface and looked, red-eyed, and hostile, at the boys.

Swamp creatures with soft fur and frightened eyes crouched on fallen trees and scanned the deck as a possible refuge. To make the scene more desolate still, if possible, two round-eyed owls answered each other's cries from a near-by cypress.

"Say," Jule whispered to Clay, during a little lull in the rain, "there's a man by that tree. I've been watching him a long time. Look at him!"

Clay followed the line of the pointing finger and laughed.

"Why, that's a bear!" he shouted. "A swamp bear—one of the kind Teddy Roosevelt came down here to shoot when he was president! Let him alone and he'll let us alone. They fight like devils when wounded or molested."

The boys all agreed to let the bear alone, but Captain Joe and Teddy seemed to have notions of hospitality. The dog barked invitingly, and Teddy did a stunt of bear talk which brought the wanderer one tree nearer to the boat. He was now in the circle of light, and could get no nearer without swimming.

"He sees Teddy and wants to ask his advice!" Jule laughed.

At that moment Mose, noting that the boys were gazing fixedly in one direction, turned his eyes that way and saw the bear. The shriek he let out might, it seemed, have been heard in New Orleans, if the wind had been blowing in that direction!

"Ah's a gone coon!" he wailed, after that one yell. "Ah's a goin' whar de good niggers go! Good bear! Good bear!" he added coaxingly.

The bear looked upon the scene for a moment longer with disapproving eyes and then turned away. For a moment he was seen walking on jammed logs, alternately wading through shallow places, and then he was lost in the darkness.

"There!" Alex. called out to Mose, "you've frightened our bear off!"

"Dat yo' bear?" asked Mose. "Den yo' keep yo' animile out our ya'd!"

Although frequently invited to return to the boat, Mose insisted on keeping his place in the tree. Now and then he called out that a bear or a deer was about to board the Rambler, but for the most part he sat still, looking about for more things to be frightened at!

The Rambler was now securely fastened in between the two trees, standing on a level, or floating on a level, rather. There was considerable water under the deck, it having worked its way down through the joints about the hatches, and the boys proceeded to lift all available covers and bail it out.

"How are we ever going to get out of here?" asked Jule, working away with a basin and a sponge. "These trees will hold us forever."

"We'll have to cut them down, Silly!" answered Case. "Just as soon as the water goes down, we'll crawl out on one of the mattresses and fix the propellers."

"Mattresses!" answered Jule. "They drifted away long ago."

"Look ahead and see," remarked Case, and Jule did so.

The willow and brake mattresses which had been towed down stream were loose from the motor boat, but they were in sight, having lodged against the mud bank farther in the swamp. They could be reached, the boys figured, by a little wading after the flood subsided, which it was certain to do before long.

"You see," Case went on, "the trees will hold the boat up, like it was in a dry dock, and we can fix the propellers and the leak and then chop down the trees and get out. Perhaps we can follow this channel out to the river. If there wasn't an opening somewhere, the current here wouldn't be so fierce!"

"There may be a channel," Clay agreed, "but if there is it must be full of standing trees and hidden snags. If we ever get out of here, we'd better run back to the main channel, and keep out of such holes in future!"

"There wouldn't be any fun in river trips," laughed Alex., swinging an axe at the head of a water snake which was trying to get up on the deck, "if it wasn't for the adventure there is in it! I wouldn't have missed this for anything!"

With the last word of this endorsement of the situation on his lips Alex. took a header over the gunwale of the boat into the water! A great trunk had bunted the Rambler on the port side, and she had tipped so as to knock the boy off his feet and over the railing before he could make up his mind what was coming off!

"Wow!" cried Clay, as the boy came, spluttering to the surface.

"You wouldn't miss this for anything!" roared Case.

"Bring a couple of snakes and an alligator out with you!" requested Jule.

Mose, sitting on the limb, high up in the tree, called down to the boy that a water snake was trying to get into his pocket, and that an alligator was nosing about his leg.

Disregarding all comment and advice, Alex. crawled back on deck and sat looking wrathfully into the flood. But his anger did not last long.

"If that log hadn't come along," he said, "I should have forgotten my bath. When it comes daylight, I'm going to get up a race with that alligator, with the snake as referee! Mose can enter if he wants to!"

Mose shivered at the thought. He was now climbing higher. When near the top he gave another yell and hustled down to a lower limb, where he sat with his hands clinging tightly to the trunk.

"Fo' de Lawd's sake!" he shrieked.

"What is it now?" asked Jule. "If you don't come down I'll shoot you!"

Mose pointed to the rim of the light zone and cried that the river robbers had come to get the boat. The boys looked where he pointed and saw three young men standing in a submerged grove of cypress trees. All were armed and all were bearded and forbidding in appearance. As the boys looked one stepped forward.

"Just a second," Clay called. "That is near enough!"

CHAPTER XX—THE DARKEY UP THE TREE

While Case talked with the young man Clay went back into the cabin to talk with Alex., who was now changing into dry clothing.

"Do you think the story that man is telling is all right?" he asked.

"I think he is telling the truth about the river thieves," Alex. replied.

"I was wondering if that wasn't just a bait to help them get on board."

"It may be, but there are river robbers in this section. They told us that where we bought the gasoline. These may be the robbers, for all I know, but we ought to make sure of that before turning them down. They'll starve here, if they have lost their boat and provisions. Of course they can get wild game, but I don't see how they are going to cook it. We ought to give them a chance, anyway."

Clay went back to the deck and listened to the conversation between Case and the visitor, who seemed a little annoyed at the doubting of his word.

"Where did you live in Chicago?" he heard Case ask.

"In furnished rooms on Elizabeth street, near Washington boulevard," was the reply.

"Where did you work?" was the next question, impertinent and personal, but seemingly necessary at that time.

"At a machine shop on Clinton street, not far from West Madison.

"Then you are machinists?"

"Yes, all of us. Business is dull in our line just now, and we thought we'd make a hit with ourselves by spending a winter in the south."

"When did you leave Chicago?"

"We left Chicago last September," answered the man, turning toward the rail. "We expect to get back sometime during the next century, if all Chicago boys are as hospitable as you are! Now, with your permission, I'll go back to my friends."

"How do you know we are from Chicago?" asked Clay, stepping forward.

The other laughed lightly and pointed to the boat's name on articles scattered about.

"But, aside from that," he said, "we'd know you anywhere. The Chicago newspapers carried a lot of feature stuff about your boat and your trips."

"All right, stranger," one of the three answered, in rather a pleasant tone of voice. "Just as you say!"

"What do you want?" asked Alex., still shivering from his cold bath.

"We want a ride out of this consarned swamp," was the reply.

"How did you get in here?" asked Clay. "Get out the way you got in!" he added.

"Our shanty boat is smashed to flinders and our grub is gone," complained the other. "It don't look as if we could walk out of here, does it?"

"Was that your fire we saw?" asked Case, drawing closer to the gunwale.

"We had a fire before the flood pounced down upon us," was the reply.

"What shall we do?" asked Clay, facing the others. "If they are on the square we can't leave them here. They would starve!"

"They may be pirates!" suggested Jule.

"I don't believe it," Case declared. "They don't look the part. Besides, if they had designs on the boat, they could have picked us off in the darkness, and we'd never have known where the bullets came from. They're all right!"

"One of you come aboard," Clay instructed, "and we'll see what you look like."

In plain view of the boys the man who had done the talking handed his gun to a companion and struck out for the boat, walking on logs part of the way, wading part of the way, and swimming when he could do neither. In a moment he was on deck.

"The three of us," he explained, "were out of work at Chicago. We had a little cash, and decided to come down here and spend the winter where we wouldn't have room-rent or restaurant bills to pay. We thought we could cut and market enough fish-poles out of the brake swamps to pay our way back in the spring."

"That wasn't a bad idea!" Jule declared.

"We were getting along all right," the other went on, "until the river thieves began troubling us. They stole our food, and at last began stealing our poles. We were getting ready to go out when the flood smashed our shanty boat into smithereens. Now we are up against it, unless you take us with you. And," he added, with a quick glance around, "you'd better take us on board, for the thieves are back there in the swamp, with their envious eyes fixed on this boat. They are mostly negroes, and escaped convicts."

"You ought to know that we've got to be careful," Clay said, as the man was about to leave the boat. "We don't know anything about you, except what you have told us, but we're going to take a chance on you. Tell your friends to come on board."

In five minutes the three were in the cabin, trying on some of Clay's clothes, for their own were not only wet but they oozed black muck. When they were dressed again they passed their revolvers over to Clay, with the statement that they wouldn't need them unless the river pirates took a hand in the game that night.

"Have the ruffians been here long?" asked Clay.

"About a month ago," was the reply, "a lot of negroes broke away from a convict camp off to the west somewhere. They came into this swamp and built a camp on a knoll, which must, by the way, be under water now. They are murderers, housebreakers and sneak thieves of the most desperate kind. We tried to make friends with them, but it was of no use. They think their camp is unknown, and so object to our getting out and telling where it is. I half believe they will try to keep you from getting out for the same reason."

"If it is all the same to you boys," another of the visitors said, "we'd like something to eat. We were half starved when we came on board. I think I can catch a fish or shoot a duck, so our supper won't cost you anything only the bother of having us around. What do you say? Do we eat?"

"I should say so!" cried Alex., sticking his head out of the cabin, "and when you are out after game get enough for me a little lunch. I haven't had anything to eat since dark!"

"Is that rowboat at the side all right?" asked the visitor, pointing to the boat which had been found up the river. "If it is, I'll get a little ways from the motor boat, in the shadows, and see what I can do getting ducks."

"The boat is all right," Alex. answered, "and I'll go with you. I'm beginning to feel the lack of adventure. I get awfully tired of this monotony sometimes!"

They all laughed at the idea of there being any monotony in the situation, there in the swamp, with the river roaring around them and the watchful thieves in the thicket, and Alex. seemed quite annoyed at the thought that they regarded his remark as a joke.

"Perhaps something will happen before you get back," Clay grinned.

"The boat may smash," said Jule, cheerfully. "It has been banged about quite a lot since we got it. Or you may find some of the robbers. There's no knowing what streak of good luck you may get into!"

"I'm not looking for any good luck of that kind!" the visitor said, as he drew the rowboat around and clambered into it. "I've had all the cheerful incidents of that character I care to have. When I get back to Chicago, I'm going to get a room next to the Desplaines street police station and go to bed at seven o'clock every night."

"What's your name?" asked Alex., abruptly as he pushed off from the Rambler.

"Gregg Holder," was the reply. "I'm just Gregg to all my friends, but I'm Bully Gregg on South Halstead street. The others are Eddie Butler and Hank Quinn."

"That settles it!" grinned Alex. "I'm going back."

"What for?" asked Gregg, in surprise. "Don't you want a duck or a fish?"

"Sure I do," was the reply, "but I'm afraid! You're the man that fought Murphy to a draw? What? And Eddie Butler is the boy that bested Murray!"

"You've got that right, kid," was the reply. "We've all been in the prize ring, but we're no slum toughs. If you think the bears and snakes and robbers are better company than we are," he added, "we'll get out of your boat!"

"You're just the lads to give the pirates a good drubbing!" Alex. laughed, "and so we'll ask you to remain with us and learn something of the rules of polite society! Let me take one oar, unless you want to keep on going round in a circle!"

"There's something pulling on the boat," Gregg said. "I can't keep it on a straight line. See if you can find out what has tangled us."

Alex. turned on his searchlight and cast its rays on the water ahead. Then he dropped his light in the bottom of the boat and stuck his hands out straight. Gregg looked up as the light fell, then dropped the oars and stuck his hands out straight!

"This is the adventure you wanted!" Gregg said, as half a dozen negroes showed on a hummock only a few feet away. "We're held up by the river thieves!"

"What do you fellows want?" Alex. demanded, looking straight into the muzzle of a gun that seemed to have a bore as large as the Hudson river tunnel.

"We want that boat, so we can get on board the motor contraption," said a voice.

"That's no negro!" whispered Alex. "It is a white man blacked up!"

"Right you are!" replied Gregg.

"What are you boys talking about?" demanded the holder of the threatening gun.

"We were telling each other how glad we were to meet you!" Alex. snarled.

"You're a nervy kid, anyhow," said the other. "Push the boat up here, so we can get in. We were raised as pets, and don't want to get wet."

There was nothing to do but obey instructions. They knew the desperate character of the men they were facing. If they followed orders and waited for an opportunity to turn the tables on their captors, they might get out of the mess with whole skins, but if they forced a fight there and then there would be little hope for them. When there were four of the pirates in the boat, crouching down under the gunwales, who made the fifth, the spokesman gave his orders.

"Now you boys row back. When we get close up I'll show myself and put the whole party under cover. See? My men will also have their guns, and if you disobey instructions in the slightest particular, you'll be shot in the back."

"That's where you like to shoot, I take it!" growled Gregg. "If I had one of you out on the bank I'd break him in two pieces and feed him to the snakes."

"Cuss if you want to!" commented the robber. "We can settle all that after a time. Just now, get over to that boat, and call out that you've found another castaway in the swamp! We'll be on board before they can say a word."

This looked like turning the Rambler over to thieves, but there was no way in which the boys could reverse conditions just then, so they rowed toward the motor boat, calling out that they had found a sick man in the jungle. The robber prodded them with the muzzle of his gun when they did not give the right inflection to their voices.

When the boat entered the circle of light the boys on board the Rambler were all leaning over the gunwale, looking for the boys and the rescued individual. There were no weapons in sight, and Alex. feared that all the revolvers were stowed away in the cabin, and that the Rambler would be taken without a shot being fired in her defense.

When the boat touched the hull of the Rambler the robber sprang to his feet, presenting two long guns as he did so.

"I'll empty these guns into the crowd of you," he said, in a low, even voice, "if there is one move on deck. We are coming aboard, and the better you use us the better we shall use you. Just sit still, boys," he added, addressing his men, "until I get on deck."

He was lithe and strong, and was on the deck in an instant, without opposition, his guns threatening the amazed boys and their visitors. Captain Joe gave forth a volley of ugly growls, and would have attacked the man, but Clay ordered him back.

"Never mind the dog," he said. "He won't bite!"

"If he does, he'll get a chance to bite lead!" the robber exclaimed. "Now, men," he went on, "climb up into the boat. Leave the rowers where they are."

Four husky negroes, all with traces of whisky in their breath, began climbing over Alex. and Gregg to reach the motor boat. As they were steadying the rocking craft, they carried no weapons in their hands.

Then something happened which was as much of a surprise to the boys as it was to the men who were trying to capture the Rambler!

A rope with a wide noose at one end came whirling out of the sky and fell over the robber's head, resting for an instant in a neat coil on his shoulders!

He clutched his weapons closer and looked up. Then the line tightened about his muscular neck until his feet left the deck and his face grew red with the blood of strangulation, then grew white. The revolvers clattered to the floor, and the man's figure toppled and fell as the rope slacked.

When this strange thing happened, Alex. and Gregg were bending their heads down to permit the negroes to clamber over them. Still they saw the rope fall, saw the man gasp as it closed about his neck, and felt the negroes springing back in dismay.

Then they arose with their heavy oars in their hands and struck slashing, crunching blows at the heads below them! One negro lifted an arm to shoot, but it fell with the bones of the shoulder crushed to pulp. One by one they dropped out of the boat, some with broken arms, some with broken heads. After they had all disappeared, either under the surface of the lagoon or into the darkness of the swamp, a shrill voice came from the tree where Mose had taken refuge from the snakes and the alligators:

"Go on, white folks," it said, "Ah goin' hang dis immitation coon up on dis tree!"

CHAPTER XXI – DODGING A POLICE BOAT

"You little coon!" Clay gasped.

"Hurrah for Mose!" cried Alex.

"If you'll come down here I'll hug you!" shouted Gregg.

"How did you ever think of it?" Case called out.

Mose, now the happiest little negro boy in the United States, sat astride of his limb and grinned until it seemed that the top of his head would drop off backward!

In the meantime, the river pirate had remained unnoticed on the deck, the rope so deftly dropped by Mose still around his neck. Case finally bent over him.

"Why!" he exclaimed, shrinking back. "The man is dead!"

"Dead!" echoed Clay. "What killed him?"

Then they all bent over the still figure for a closer examination. Just as Case had declared, the robber was dead. His neck had been broken by the rope when Mose had drawn him off his feet! Alex. looked up at the boy.

"You must have a good pull in your arms!" he cried. "How did you manage to swing him up? You're a wonder, Mose!"

Mose only grinned in reply, but Clay explained the matter by saying that the boy had thrown the rope over a limb higher up and used that as a pulley.

"Still," he added, "it took a lot of muscle to jerk that heavy man off his feet. I didn't think the boy had it in him."

Then came the question as to what disposition should be made of the body. There was no hard ground near at hand so that a decent grave could be prepared. There were marshy knolls, it is true, but any excavation made there would instantly fill with water.

"Well," Gregg said, "the best we can do is to bury him in the water. I don't mean in the lagoon or in the river, but in a grave which will fill with water. There he will at least be out of the reach of reptiles and wild animals when the water subsides."

"But how are we ever going to get out there and dig a grave?" asked Jule, who was not inclined to waste much effort on the body of a man who, in life, would have robbed, perhaps murdered, them!

"With your permission," Gregg said, "we'll take the body out and bury it. I haven't much use for men of his type, but he's dead, and that settles all accounts!"

"We may be able to get a couple of birds for supper while we are away," suggested Eddie Butler. "We have been so busy lately, that we haven't eaten, or provided anything to eat! I'm empty clear to my toes!"

"And I'll catch a fish off the boat!" Jule volunteered. "I saw some big ones jumping up not long ago! They've been driven out of their nests by the flood."

So Gregg and his friends went away in the rowboat to bury the outlaw and get a couple of ducks for supper, while Jule and Alex. angled over the stern of the boat for a fish. The first rush of the flood was past, but the water was still high. There was a strong current rushing past the stern of the Rambler, and this indicated that there must be a channel open to the main river not far below.

The boys caught a great catfish and two awkward-looking buffalo-fish and turned them loose in the stream before they succeeded in getting anything they wanted for supper. Then they caught a dozen perch of good size and proceeded to clean them.

By the time the fish were ready for the pan Gregg and his friends were back from their expedition with half a dozen fat ducks, already dressed.

"We'll have some for breakfast, and some for dinner!" Eddie declared. "I feel now as if I'd never get enough to fill me up again!"

Something long and twisting dropped on the man's shoulders and fell off to the deck.

"Holy smoke!" he shouted. "Look at the snake!"

A shout from up the tree told of the trick Mose had played on the man, and the rope was coiled away. In a short time Mose came sliding down the trunk.

"He smells supper!" explained Clay. "I've a notion to set Captain Joe on him!"

"Dat dog don't bite dis coon!" Mose replied. "Ah'm in lub wid dat dog!"

Captain Joe and Teddy came forward and looked the three visitors over approvingly.

"That bear would make a good meal!" Gregg declared, with a wink at Case.

Mose's eyes stuck out for a minute, and then he tickled his own chin and gave out a sound like a goat.

"B-a-a-a-a-a-a! B-a-a-a-a-a-a-a-a!" he bleated.

"What's the matter with the coon?" asked Gregg, with a look of surprise.

"He's telling us to get wise to the alfalfa!" Jule cut in. "Alex. don't know how to translate so white men can understand."

"You'll both wash dishes for a month!" roared Clay, doubled over with laughter. "We make that a penalty for talking slang," he explained, turning to Gregg.

"But I don't understand yet," the other went on. "What is the matter with the boy? Has he turned himself into a billy goat?"

"He's suggesting that you mow the lawn!" Case explained. "He doesn't like the fire-escapes!"

Clay roared and pointed to the beards worn by the three, and then they understood and joined in the laugh until the swamp echoed back the sounds.

"You'll all have to wash dishes, I take it!" Gregg declared.

"That's about the way it usually turns out, when one starts talking slang," Clay explained. "We're all so full of it that it just bubbles out."

"It is fine that we have something to be jolly over," Gregg hastened to say, "for the prospects of getting out of here are not alluring."

"Wouldn't be no fun if everything went right!" Alex. insisted. "We have the most sport when we're lost, or stolen, or strayed away. Now, you watch me cook these ducks."

The boy got out a baking pan standing on three short legs. The bottom was double so as to prevent burning. Then he put two fat ducks inside, secured the cover, and removed what seemed to Gregg to be the whole top of the stove.

The short legs of the pan rested on the red-hot coals in the firebox, while the cover was always within reach. As soon as the ducks, which had previously been hastily parboiled, began to simmer and send forth appetizing odors, the boy watched them every minute, turning and basting until they were a beautiful golden brown.

In the meantime coffee had been made and the fish fried on the electric coil.

"I presume you'll want hot biscuits for supper, too?" asked Clay.

The visitors were too busy with the game to do more than shake their heads.

"We usually have three kinds of meat, fish, baked potatoes, pancakes, light bread, pie, honey, and three or four vegetables on the side," Alex. explained, with a wink at Mose, who sat in a corner next to the deck with Joe and Teddy watching the meat disappearing from a "drumstick" he was busily engaged on.

"An' possum pie!" the little negro boy added, licking his chops.

"Sure! I forgot the possum pie!" Alex. declared. "Excuse me!"

"Certainly!" laughed Gregg, "and we'll excuse you, too, for all future products of the imagination! The twenty course dinners at the La Salle haven't got anything on this little banquet! For my part, I don't care whether we ever get out of here, now, or not."

"Some day," Alex. observed, "I'll show you how to cook a steak à la brigand! After you eat one of them you'll go hungry for a week before you'll touch anything else!"

"You may lead me to one of them any time you see fit!" Eddie laughed.

The river was still roaring and foaming about the Rambler, caught in the narrow space between the two cypress trees. Just where the boat lay the current turned away to the east, that is the current of the lagoon. The Mississippi was, of course, across the inundated spit of land which lay on the west shore of the river and on the east side of the bayou or lagoon.

Just as the boys finished their somewhat delayed supper the lights of a steamer showed up the stream. It passed the mouth of the bayou and hugged the opposite shore of the Mississippi for a time, then headed for the west shore.

"That's strange!" Case exclaimed. "She sees our lights, but what is she coming over to this side for?"

The mystery became more of a mystery still when, reaching the west side, the steamer turned prow up stream and started to breast the flood, still carrying great masses of wreckage down stream. She made her way up to the mouth of the bayou and stopped, her propellers going just fast enough to keep from dropping back.

"If I'm not mistaken," Gregg suggested, "that is a boat carrying officers on a hunt for the escaped convicts. Can't we get out of here before they reach us?"

"Why should we run away from them?" asked Clay, suspiciously.

"Because they will mistake us for convicts," replied Gregg. "An officer in a position to abuse his authority always does so. Many of the man-hunters along the river are little better than the men they hunt. Some of them are worse. This, of course, does not apply to the sheriffs and deputies of the counties touching the river, but to hired detectives and gunmen who come here to make a living hunting others."

"You must be sore on the police," Alex. exploded. "I've got a lot of friends on the Chicago police force. They're good fellows, at that!"

"All right!" Gregg assented. "There are a lot of good men there. But if you want to remain here and permit those ruffians to overrun your boat, insult you, and hold you prisoners until you can get to some town where identification is possible, you can do so. We can stand it if you can."

"There may be some sense in what he says," Clay urged, "and if we could get out of the trap we are in and make the propellers go, I'd be willing to go on down the river and let the officers have the whole country to themselves."

"Can't we follow this bayou current and get out on the river below them?" asked Jule.

Clay said no; Gregg and his chums said yes.

"The water has been cutting a channel for a long time," Gregg explained. "It needed only a slight push to send the remaining bank down. There are few obstructions in the new channel, as I figure it out, and I believe we would go through like a top once we got started. And we'd better hurry, if we are going to do anything, for, of course, they have seen your lights. They wouldn't have stopped here if they hadn't."

"But the propellers!" urged Clay. "They're broken."

In a moment one of the men had his clothes off to the undersuit and was diving down at the stern of the Rambler. He remained under the water so long that the boys began to fear that he had met with some accident, or been attacked by a snake or an alligator. He came up smiling, however.

"Only clogged!" he cried. "You, Gregg and Eddie, get axes and chop the east tree down! The boat will then swing away from the other. You must make the cut down in the water, then we'll have to lift the prow over the stump."

The plan suggested proved successful, and the Rambler, under power, and trailing the mattresses, was soon feeling her way down the new channel. Then excitement was observed on the steamer, and she was headed about for the main stream again. It looked like a race was on!

CHAPTER XXII — THE SHERIFF KNOWS A LOT

It was still raining when the Rambler headed into the Mississippi, and there was no glimmer of light in sight save that which came from the steamer, still puffing at the mouth of the bayou, and that which lighted the path of the motor boat. The wind had gone down, and the slow, soft rain dominated the night.

It was evident from the very start that the steamer was no match for the Rambler when it came to a question of speed. As well might a delivery truck attempt to compete in swiftness with a perfect touring car.

Besides the power of speed, the Rambler had another quality which enabled her to rapidly increase the distance between the two boats. The river was still covered with wreckage, and the motor boat was a good dodger! She responded quickly to her helm, avoiding the driftwood ahead easily, while the steamer was slower in picking her way.

"Your boat is a peach!" Gregg exclaimed, enthusiastically, as the lights of the steamer dropped out of sight behind a bend in the river. "Nothing would please me better than a long trip in her."

"Well," Clay replied, "why not? We are going to the Gulf, and are in no hurry to get there. We are shy sleeping bunks, but if you boys can put up with beds on the floor you are welcome to go along with us. I reckon you'll manage to supply your share of the provisions!"

"The prospect is an attractive one," Gregg replied, "but I think we'd better stop at Vicksburg and find employment of some kind. Later, we may go on down the river in a houseboat of our own. That depends on how lucky we are in getting good jobs."

"We shall be sorry to part with you," Case put in. "We have been together only a few hours, but a great deal has happened in that time! Only for your warning, the river thieves might have sneaked aboard the Rambler and captured it. In that case, you know very well what would have become of us. We should have been murdered!"

"I have no doubt that you would have taken care of yourselves," Eddie declared.

"There's one thing I want to ask you," Clay went on, "and that is about the outlaw you buried back in the swamp. He was a white man, wasn't he?"

"Yes; a white man blacked up like a negro."

"Did you look him over carefully enough to be able to give me a description of him?"

"Well, we washed him up a little when we saw that he was a Caucasian, and I got a fair impression of his face, which wasn't a prepossessing one, by any means."

"Can you give me something of a notion of it in a few words?" asked Clay.

"Some old acquaintance of yours?" asked the other, with a smile at Case.

"He might have been. The fact is, I thought I recognized the voice of the spokesman."

"There!" Alex. exclaimed. "I had that same notion. Mose," he added, turning to the negro boy, "was that the man who threw you and the dog into the water?"

"Ah sure done thought so!" was the reply.

"You think it was Sam, the Robber, the man who accompanied Red?" asked Jule.

"I didn't know but it might be!" answered Clay, and Alex. at once insisted that it was the same man. Mose was ready to swear to the fellow's identity by this time!

"Tell us how he looked after the black was washed off," requested Clay, after a short pause, during which the three men compared notes — mental notes — of their impressions of the man they had left in the lonely grave in the swamp.

"We have decided on one word that expresses our thought of the man," Gregg finally replied. "You know that all human beings in some manner resemble some wild animal species. Some men are lions, some are monkeys, some are dogs, some are bears, some are foxes. Well, this man was a fox!"

"I thought so," Clay exclaimed. "I thought the fellow's voice sounded like Sam's."

"There are many men with fox-faces," Gregg warned. "This man may not have been the individual you refer to as Sam. If he is an enemy of yours, keep looking for him."

With this bit of good advice the matter was dropped for the time. The steamer was no longer in sight, but the Rambler was kept on her way to the Gulf.

In the middle of the next forenoon they came to Delta, which is at the bottom of the Vicksburg cutoff, on the west bank of the river. Here, with many handshakes and expressions of regret at parting, the three men left the boat.

"If we have any luck at all," Gregg said, as the Rambler pushed out, "we'll meet you somewhere south of New Orleans. We've always wanted to see that swamp country."

The boys moved slowly down the river after that.

Again they were enjoying themselves, fishing, hunting and exploring the country on either side of the great stream.

There were lowlands, swamps, winding bayous and forests in places. Again, there were plantations, with noble houses showing from the river. Whenever they halted at a plantation landing they were received most hospitably.

The wreckage of the flood was running out of the stream, and the water was dropping down to normal. Occasionally they left the boat at night and built rousing camp-fires on high banks. At such times plantation hands often gathered about them with banjo and mandolin and violin and made the night musical.

They heard no mention of the Rock Island warehouse robbery until they approached Baton Rouge. The night before they sighted that beautiful city they camped on a piece of high land on a small island. No sooner was their fire blazing high than a couple of rowboats skimmed across the river and drew up near the little camp.

There were three men in one boat and two in the other, and the whole five hastened to greet the boys. They were evidently planters, for they were well dressed and gave the impression of being gentlemen.

The man who seemed to be the leader looked keenly around the camp, peered into the cabin of the Rambler, and then approached Clay with outstretched hand.

"I don't need to ask who you boys are," he laughed. "I am a regular reader of the Chicago newspapers. One of them, not long ago, printed your pictures, including those of the dog and the cub! If you'll desert this camp and come over to the house, I'll be glad to put you up for the night."

"I hardly think we would sleep well under a roof," Clay laughed, "but we're all very thankful for your kindness. Besides, we'll have to remain here and watch the boat. We've had some trouble coming down, and are determined to be on our guard."

"You won't find any river thieves around here," smiled the visitor. "I'm sheriff of this parish, and I've taken considerable trouble to clear the country of them. You say you've had trouble on the way down? Then this must be the party that gave the officers such a race up above Vicksburg?"

"There was a steamer chased us — for a little while!" grinned Clay.

"Yes, I understand," replied the sheriff. "The newspapers were full of the incident the next day, and you were held forth to the public as the boldest of river brigands! Why did you run away from the officers?"

"We only suspected that they were officers," was the answer.

"It wouldn't have taken long for you to have found out," smiled the officer.

"It might have taken us a long time to get away from them," Clay answered. "You know how eager some officers are to make a capture.

Well, we didn't want to be bothered with them, so we just took to our heels."

"The officers were looking for a boy believed to be on your boat," the sheriff remarked. "They had information that he had been seen with you on two occasions."

"He must refer to Chet Vinton," Case interrupted.

"I don't know his name," the sheriff went on, "but he is the boy believed to have taken a hand in the Rock Island robbery."

"That is the lad," Clay answered, with an amused smile. "We have had him on board the Rambler on two occasions, and each time he has mysteriously disappeared."

"Where did you see him last?"

"At Memphis."

"That was after you rented a deposit box at a bank?"

"You seem to know all about it," grinned Clay. "Yes, he left soon after I rented the deposit box in the bank. By the way, do you know a giant of a man, red-headed and kind-hearted, who is a gentleman of leisure one moment and a river pirate the next?"

Clay thought he saw suppressed excitement in the face of the sheriff as he asked the question, and waited expectantly for an answer. The officer hesitated before saying a word, then he pushed the direct question aside.

"There are a good many men along the river who might answer to the description," he said, "but I can't call any names to mind just now. What about him?"

"Why, I met him on the river," Clay answered, resolved to be just as secretive as the officer, "and I also met a man I took to be him at Memphis. I have a notion that I would like to meet him again some time. He's all right, that man!"

"Tell me this," said the sheriff, then, "what did you boys discover in the old house on the bank of the lagoon? I understand that at least two of your party spent the day there. I'd like to know what they saw and heard in the house."

Clay regarded the sheriff suspiciously.

"Has there anything happened to us on this trip that you don't know about?" he asked, then.

"Why," replied the other, "we've been hearing about you all down the river. Don't forget that we have telegraph wires in this country, as well as up north. Yes, we've heard a lot about you, and, to tell the truth, I've been waiting rather anxiously for you to make your appearance. What about the old mansion, where the negro boy and the dog got your friends out of a bad mess?"

"Say," Alex., who had been listening, cut in, "what do you know about that old mansion? What kind of a gang is it that holds forth there?"

"You ought to know!" smiled the sheriff. "You called on them."

"Yes, and they insisted on our making a longer visit!" grinned Alex.

"Now, what is it about the boy?" the sheriff said, changing the subject.

"You know all that I know about him," replied Clay. "He ran away from us following the visit to the boat of the bank cashier and two friends."

"Yes, I heard about that," said the officer. "Now, will you be good enough to tell me if you have seen him since that night?"

"We have not, except that he returned to the Rambler during the dark hours and restored something he had taken away from her."

"Are you sure it was the boy who came back with the leather bag?" asked the sheriff, with a most exasperating laugh. "Are you sure it was the boy?"

"I am not," Clay answered, wonderingly. "I spoke too hastily. Come, Mr. Sheriff, tell me how you know anything about that leather bag."

"I don't know much about it, that's the trouble," was the reply. "I wish I knew more. Now, tell me this: Have you an appointment with this boy farther down the river? Do you expect to meet him again during your trip?"

Clay replied that he hoped to, and the sheriff said little more on the subject. He expected the sheriff to ask for the key to the deposit box, but he did not.

CHAPTER XXIII – A NIGHT IN NEW ORLEANS

"I believe," Clay declared, after a long pause, during which the voices of negroes along the levee came softly through the night, "that you know something about the three persons we are just now interested in."

"Name the three," laughed the sheriff. "Who are they?"

"First, the man we have always called Red, the Robber."

"You have referred to him before, my boy."

"But you gave me no satisfaction," urged Clay, eagerly. "Do you know him?"

"I have heard of a man who sometimes answers to the name of Red. What next?"

"The boy, Chester Vinton, accused of having had a hand in the Rock Island robbery."

"Why do you think I know anything of him? If I knew where he was I'd be sure and keep him long enough to find out what he knows about that robbery!"

"And the third person is the cashier of the bank where I left the packet. What did he come on board the Rambler for? Who were the men with him?"

"The cashier said he was curious to see the famous boat, didn't he?"

"Pshaw!" exclaimed Clay. "That wasn't the reason he came on board! Honest, now, didn't he expect to find some of the plunder taken from the warehouse on the boat?"

"I don't know what he expected to find, I'm sure. I have never talked with him."

"Now," Clay went on, "you have referred to the leather bag, the one thrown on the deck of the Rambler. Who told you about the bag if the cashier didn't? I begin to think the cashier took the bag and threw it back, or caused it to be thrown back, when he discovered that it contained nothing of value."

142

"What did it contain when you first saw it?" asked the sheriff, a twinkle in his eyes. "Let us talk about that, for a time!"

"I'm going to show you," Clay replied, half angrily, "that I can be just as secretive as you can! I don't know anything about the leather bag!"

"Well," the officer went on, with a puzzling expression on his face, "if you come across this boy Chet will you let me know about it?"

"No, I won't!" replied Clay.

"That's right! Speak right up, promptly! Now I know just what to ' expect!"

"You might clear up the whole matter," Clay complained, "and yet you won't open your mouth! I'm not going to assist you—not if I get a chance, which is doubtful."

"Well," said the sheriff, moving toward the boats, "I must be getting along! I may see you later. If you come back this way don't forget that you are all to be my guests for a few days. I really want to get better acquainted with you boys."

"We'll think it over," laughed Clay. "We're thankful for the invitation, anyway."

"And when you get down below New Orleans," the officer suggested, "look out for the real thing in pirates! That boat of yours would make a fine craft for a freebooter. And human life is not regarded as very valuable down there."

"We'll be careful, thank you!" Clay answered, and the sheriff and his men went off in their boats, leaving the boys looking wonderingly at their retreating forms.

"Now," Alex. grumbled, "what did they come here for, anyway? They simply let us know that they were wise to our troubles and went away—without finding out anything, or giving us any information except that they were acquainted with our movements."

"They did ask for the boy Chet," suggested Case.

"Don't you suppose they know what it was I put in the deposit box at the bank?" asked Clay. "Of course they know! Now, why didn't the sheriff demand the key and claim the diamonds as stolen property?"

"It is peaches to prunes that he has opened the box long before this, or that some one has!" Alex. put in. "He's the original little pry-in!"

"I'm all out of guesses," Jule declared, "and so I'm going to bed."

The boys saw nothing of the sheriff the next morning. They were on their way at an early hour, and, going at a swift clip, were within sight of New Orleans by nightfall.

"Shall we spend the night in the city?" asked Case, then.

"And where would we leave the Rambler?" asked Jule. "If we left it on the river we wouldn't have any boat in the morning."

Without deciding the point the boys tied up some distance above the city and prepared supper. The moon arose in a clear sky about eight o'clock and the boys did not turn on the electric lights after eating. They sat in the moonlight on the deck and watched Captain Joe, Teddy and Mose tumbling about.

"If it wasn't so much trouble to dress," Case said, after a time, "I'd like to go to a theatre to-night, and have a swell supper afterwards."

"You don't want much!" laughed Clay.

"Why not go, then?" asked Alex. "I'm not too lazy to put on a decent suit."

"Do you mean it?" demanded Case, rising from his chair.

"If the others will stay and guard the boat I mean it," was the reply.

"Go if you want to," Clay answered the inquiring look, "for Jule and Mose can help me keep off the pirates! Only don't remain away all night."

"Ah done like to see dis town!" Mose suggested.

"You'll have to wait until some other time, Mose," Clay replied. "You must stay on board and help repel boarders now!"

The little negro grinned as if perfectly satisfied with the arrangement, and went on with his boxing match with Teddy. Case and Alex. dressed as rapidly as possible and were taken ashore, in the four-oared boat captured above Memphis, at the foot of a street not far from a trolley line running to the business center of the city. When Clay returned with the rowboat, Mose was on one of the willow mattresses which had been brought down the river.

In a few minutes Clay called to him to come on board, but there was no reply. Mose was nowhere in sight. He had evidently started out to see the city on his own hook!

"I reckon that is the last we'll ever see of him," Jule commented, as they gave up the search for the boy. "He'll get to shooting craps in the city and live there forever. Can't do anything with a kid like that."

"It is hard work to knock any sense into the head of a boy brought up on the St. Louis levee," Clay admitted, "but I hope he'll return."

"Perhaps he followed Case and Alex., and will return with them," Jule suggested.

"That would be like him," Clay admitted.

The boys were not sleepy and the moonlight was fine, so they sat on the deck until midnight, waiting for the others to return. They had not returned at one o'clock, and the watchers were becoming anxious when a call from the shore came to their ears. In a moment the call was repeated, shriller than before, and then there followed a splash in the river and a shot.

The boys saw a figure swimming toward the Rambler and got out their guns.

"Doesn't look very formidable!" Clay observed, as the figure came nearer. "It looks like Mose! Now, what the mischief is the little coon up to, I'd like to know?"

"It is Mose, all right," Jule assented, "and there's some one on shore shooting at him. He may have been up to some of his pranks on shore."

Directly the shooting on the shore ceased, and then Mose came on faster, not being obliged to swim under water half the time. He crawled, chilly and dripping, on deck and rolled his eyes at Clay.

"Dey done got um!" he exclaimed.

"What about it?" demanded Jule. "Who's got them?"

After much questioning it was learned that Mose had left the Rambler in time to overtake Case and Alex., that he had followed them into the city, and had seen them talking with Chet Vinton, the mysterious boy who seemed to turn up in the oddest places and to disappear in the strangest manner.

The boys had talked with Chet for a long time, the little negro said, and had not gone to the theatre at all. Instead, they had gone into a disreputable part of the city with the boy, and had there met two men believed by the negro to be thieves.

At last, at a late hour, the boy declared, still with much hesitation, Case and Alex. had attempted to leave the little cottage where they were sitting and had been forcibly detained. Chet, Mose said, had been the first one to oppose their departure. Then he, Mose, had dashed away to warn those on the boat and had been followed by some of the men he had been watching.

He described in glowing terms and very bad English how he had jumped fences and chased through moonlit backyards, and how he had been shot at at every step of the way!

"I reckon you were shot at because some one mistook you for a thief."

Mose looked reproachfully at Jule, and rolled his eyes wider than ever.

"What are we going to do now?" questioned Clay. "I don't know how much of this story to believe."

"One of us might leave the boat and go back with Mose," the other suggested.

At mention of his going back to the place from which he had fled, Mose rushed into the cabin, lowered his bunk, and covered up, head and ears, in the bedclothes! Captain Joe tried to worry him out, but without success.

"I believe the dog can find them," Clay remarked, presently.

"I'm willing to go and try what he can do," Jule answered.

146

"If we could get that foolish negro to come along!" Clay commented.

Jule went back to the bunk and shook Mose by the shoulder.

"Come on," he cried. "We're going to take Captain Joe out with us and find the boys. You'll have to go along and show the way!"

"Fo' de Law'd's sake!" wailed the boy. "Let dis coon die in hes bed!"

"Come on!" insisted Jule. "You've got to come."

After many arguments and many promises of reward in the shape of yellow shoes and red shirts, the boy consented to go ashore again. Clay warned Jule to be watchful and cautious and saw him go away with Mose and Captain Joe with a feeling that a great deal depended on his good judgment.

Jule and Mose were obliged to wait some time for a late car, and the walk to the quarter of the city toward which their steps were turned was a long one, so it was nearly three o'clock in the morning when they came to a dilapidated old shanty near the river front. Mose declared this was the place, and Captain Joe seemed to think so also, for he said quite positively, in his best dog-English, that there were people he knew in that old ruin, which was dark in every window and door.

Now and then, as the boys and the dog stood in front of the house, loiterers of the night paused in their aimless wanderings and regarded them speculatively, possibly mistaking them for disreputables like themselves. For a long time there was no sign of life in the house, and then a soft footstep was heard at the front door and the boys heard a knob stealthily turned.

Listen as they might, they heard nothing more for a long time, and then a figure dropped softly out of an open window and moved off toward the river, evidently failing to see the watchers crouched near at hand.

"That's Chet!" Jule muttered, starting away, but Mose shook his head vigorously.

CHAPTER XXIV — SOMETHING DOING ALL THE TIME

Jule was at a loss what course to pursue. The boy who had left the house might be Chet, in which case he felt that he ought to follow and induce him to return to the Rambler, if that were possible.

The diamonds which had been placed in the deposit vault belonged to Chet. At least the boy had had them in his possession when he came aboard the boat, and in the absence of any other claim upon them they belonged to him. If they did not belong to him, then their owner ought to be found. If they did, he ought to have possession of them.

Just how a boy had become possessed of a fortune in precious stones, Jule was not trying to figure out at that time. What was in his mind was the thought that the question of ownership ought to be settled at once. This question, he believed, could best be settled by the boy himself.

He waived, for the time being, all consideration of the possible connection of the gems with the Rock Island robbery, all consideration of the possible connection of the boy with the man known to him as Red, the Robber. Chet himself could best decide the question of ownership, and Jule thought he ought to be taken back to the boat, by force if necessary.

Just as the boy was on the point of pursuing the figure, now fast disappearing in the shadows along the levee, Mose pulled at his arm and pointed to Captain Joe. The dog, with short ears and tail rampant, was crouching close to the closed door of the house, uttering low growls as his paws moved toward the threshold.

"Alex. in dar!" the little negro exclaimed.

Then there came a heavy, stumbling footstep along the walk, and a burly man in the garb of a riverman paused at the door, overlooking the boys crouched at the angle of the house, but cursing the dog drunkenly. Captain Joe behaved remarkably well under the kicks delivered at him, and the newcomer took a key from his pocket and opened the door. Before he could enter the dog had disappeared in the darkness of the interior.

"I reckon Alex. is in there, perhaps Case, too," Jule muttered.

"Yo' sure cain't fool dat purp!" Mose whispered.

The boys did not attempt to follow on into the house by the open doorway, but passed on to the window and entered there. All was still dark inside. They could hear the man who had just entered moving about, still striking at and cursing the dog.

Directly another key was turned, and then all was confusion. Jule switched on his flashlight and the circle it cut in the darkness revealed the man standing in a doorway with a long-barreled revolver in one shaking hand. The casings of the doorway appeared to be of two-inch plank, and the door itself was crossed by iron bands.

The man turned as the light flashed out and fired, the bullet going wide of the mark. Then a voice came from the interior of the room, a voice which brought joy to the hearts of boys outside. The voice of Alex.

"Get him, Joe!" the voice cried. "Get him good!"

The man wheeled and shot at the springing dog, but the bullet went off into the ragged ceiling instead of into Captain Joe's head, as intended. Directly the dog and the man were in a struggle on the floor, the only light Jule's electric.

Alex. and Case came out of the room, leaping over the fighters, and seized Jule and Mose in enthusiastic embraces.

"Wait!" Jule commanded. "Get the man on the floor first. The dog will take his life. Joe!" he added, "let go!"

"Take him away!" shrieked the man. "He's chewed my arm off now!"

Jule picked up the fallen man's revolver and held it to his head while Alex. forced the dog away. There was blood on Captain Joe's jaws, and the man on the floor was breathing heavily.

"Shut the door and put down the window!" Alex. said, presently, "and put the light out! There's no more fight in this chap just now."

"Here, I'll fix him," Case said. "I'll chuck him into this refrigerator and lock him up. See how well he likes his own medicine."

"But he'll get right out!" advised Jule.

"Oh, will he!" Alex. answered. "Then he'll do more than we could. I'll bet the walls of that hole are a foot thick! And the air? I'm choked to death."

"We tried our best to get out and couldn't," Case added.

"Suppose we see if he is badly hurt before we leave him?" Jule put in.

An examination showed that the dog had seized the fellow by the shoulder and bitten through the flesh, making an ugly though not serious wound.

"That won't hurt him!" Alex. declared. "His chums will come and get him in the morning, anyway. Chuck him in and lock the door and we'll climb out of this!"

"Isn't the place watched?" asked Jule, peering out cautiously.

"It would be if the outlaws weren't drunk," Alex. replied. "There's a copper over on the other side of the street. Probably he heard the shots. We'll duck out of a back window and make for the Rambler."

The boys were watched furtively by the policemen in that section of the city as they made their way along the streets with the dog, but they were not molested. When they came to the residence district where there was little fear of their being followed, Jule turned to Alex. with a grin.

"How did you like the play?" he asked?

"You saw about as much of it as we did!" was the reply.

"How did you come to get into such a scrape?" was the next question.

"The outlaws followed us from the boat," was the answer. "Oh, yes they did," the boy insisted as Jule grinned. "They were waiting for the Rambler to come down stream! They thought we had the diamonds and were going into the city to dispose of them. They swore they'd keep us in that hole, without food or drink, until we told them where the stones were! I wish I'd never heard of the diamonds!"

"Who was the other boy?" asked Jule.

"The other boy? Where? When? Oh, that was Chet! We'll settle with him!"

"The lad who jumped out of an open window just before we got in and ducked away toward the river. Was that Chet?"

"Blessed if I know!" Alex. answered. "It might have been."

"I believe that really was Chet!" Jule declared. "It looked like him."

"How did you get here?" asked Case. "You're a wonder! And Mose and Joe, too!"

As the boys walked along the story of Mose's runaway expedition was told, and Alex. immediately grasped the little negro boy by the collar.

"You're a little brick!" he exclaimed, "and I'm going to see that you have a 'possum for dinner to-morrow — or to-day, rather — if there is one to be found in the city."

"It is a wonder," Case commented, "that the fellows didn't make an attack on the Rambler! After they searched us, they talked for a long time in whispers and then started away. I believe they did go to the boat — and Clay there alone!"

"We ought to make better time," Jule observed. "Where do we get the trolley?"

"Unless we get an owl car," Alex. replied, "we'll get none at all until the early run, and that will be after five o'clock. Guess we've got to walk it."

Eager, yet almost dreading, to learn the exact state of affairs on the motor boat, the boys traveled fast, breaking into a run now and then, much to the wonder and amazement of the few negroes they encountered making their way to the business section.

At last, just before daylight, they came in sight of the boat. A short distance up the bank a bright camp-fire was burning, and several figures could be seen moving around it. All was quiet on board the Rambler. No lights were in sight, either from the cabin or the prow. The boys waited a short time, wondering, and then Jule went to the levee and looked for the rowboat. It was not there.

"They've got possession, I reckon," he said, when he came back.

"Then all we've got to do is to take it away from them!" Alex. suggested.

"But how?" asked Jule. "We can't go on board without their seeing us."

"First," Alex. went on, "I'm going to make a sneak up to that fire and find out what those men are talking about. They may be all-right fellows, for all we know."

The others waited breathlessly for the boy's return. When he came back he said:

"They've been on board and ransacked the cabin. They found no one there! Now, what do you think has become of Clay?" he added.

"It's a wonder they didn't run off with the boat," Case said.

"Oh, they wouldn't do that," Alex. ventured. "They want to get us. I half believe the men are officers. What gets me is what they built that fire for?"

"Probably thought we were fools enough to run up to it," hazarded Jule.

"But where is Clay?" demanded Case. "We've got to find him. Do you know if they left any one on board the boat?"

"I didn't hear anything said about that," was the reply, "but it is a cinch that they did. And I believe there's more than one on board, too."

"Hard luck to lose the boat after getting so far on our journey!" Jule commented.

"We don't lose the boat, if they are officers," Alex. hastened to say. "What they want is the crew! We'll fool 'em at that. I'm going to swim over and see what's doing on board. If everything is all right, I'll make a noise like an owl."

"That's a nice long swim," Case objected. "I don't think you can make it."

"Mose made it, didn't you, coon?" Alex. replied. "I'm the boy that poured the water into the Mississippi! Nice adventure this?" he continued. "I'm going to give the residents of the valley a chromo each

152

for the manner in which we have been entertained by them! Here goes for the Rambler!"

"You act like you meant to walk back to Chicago," Case suggested, as Alex. started away, turning away from the river in order to avoid the people at the fire.

"Oh, I'm only going to walk up a little way and drift as I swim down."

"Come up on the other side, then," Case cautioned. "Then you won't be seen."

When Alex. started away on his perilous trip Mose disappeared, and Captain Joe was nowhere to be seen the next minute. Case searched and grumbled, but did not find them.

"They've gone with Alex.," he suggested. "They always do. Well, let them go, they can swim better than I can! Wish I was along, also."

"If they are officers, the men at the fire," Jule asked, "why don't we go right up to them and find out what's doing? They won't lock us up, will they?"

"That is just about what they will do if they get us," was the slow reply. "We would get out of jail in time, but who wants to lie in a cell when there is so much fun to be had on the river? These fellows have been wired to head us off, probably by the sheriff we met up there. It may be that the diamonds Clay put in the deposit box have been identified as the ones stolen from Rock Island. I wish Chet would show up right now!"

"Oh, well, if they want to coop us up," Jule agreed, "we'd better cut our luck until they find out who stole the diamonds — or, at any rate, find out that we didn't."

The boy ceased speaking suddenly, for the motor boat was getting under way, heading down toward the business wharves!

CHAPTER XXV — COMMONPLACE, AFTER ALL

"Can that be Alex. moving the Rambler?" asked Case, as the motors sputtered out their insistent clamor. "I don't believe he has had time to get on board yet."

"Well, Captain Joe has, anyway!" Jule declared, as a sharp bark came from the craft, which now seemed to be turning around. "That's the Captain's voice, all right."

Standing high on the levee, with the lights of the city growing below them, the lads watched the Rambler for a moment and then started on a run up the stream toward a small landing that was not far from the camp-fire.

"If Alex. wasn't on board," Case reasoned, "Captain Joe wouldn't be there. If Alex. is running the boat up to that landing, it is safe for us to go there."

The Rambler did tie up at the landing, and then the boys saw that the rowboat they had missed was tied to her stern. The willow mattresses were also still hanging on to the cords to which they had been tied. The men at the fire started up toward the landing as the boys reached it, but, much to the surprise of the lads, they did not attempt to go on board. In a moment Clay, Alex. and Mose showed their faces on deck.

"Come aboard!" shouted Alex. "I've arranged a surprise party for you here."

"What is Chet doing on there?" demanded Case. "I thought we left him with his new friends, the thieves, in that old house in the city."

"This is no time for story-telling!" said another voice on board, and the man who had been known as Red, the Robber, came out of the cabin and sat down, calmly, on the gunwale. The boys on shore were, by this time, prepared for almost anything. When they reached the deck, Red waved a farewell to the men on the levee and the boat whirled down toward the Gulf of Mexico.

"You see," Alex. grinned, "we don't know where we are going, but we are on our way."

154

"I know!" Clay insisted, "we are going to complete our trip to the Gulf of Mexico. We've had all the mystery we need on this voyage, and the next one that starts anything in that line will be banished to one of the mattresses!"

"All right," Alex. retorted. "We don't care about knowing what this all means! I reckon it is too commonplace to refer to again."

He grinned at Red and Chet as he spoke, and they both laughed back at him.

"We have with us to-night," Alex. went on, in a very good imitation of the after-dinner orator, "Red, the Robber! His specialty is taking boats away from boys and sneaking off down the river with them — until some one gets the drop on him!

"We also have with us," he continued, "Chester Vinton, the waif who was rescued from a barren island in the Mississippi with a hundred thousand dollars' worth of diamonds in his possession! He will soon do his stunt of telling how he found them in a piece of pie at a Rock Island restaurant.

"This wonderful Chet is also the last word in friendship. When he sees boys who have befriended him, it is his habit to turn them over to thieves, who lock them up — not in anger, but to protect them from other naughty boys!"

Instead of showing anger at this blunt talk, Red and Chet sat down on the gunwale and laughed until the river echoed back their voices. Clay also seemed much amused.

"What's the answer?" demanded Case, turning to Chet.

"Now you boys just wait a short time," Red observed, "and you'll know all about it. I would tell you right now, only I see how hungry you all are. And, seeing that I have a monster beefsteak in the cabin, with ducks ready to roast, and eggs ready to fry, why, it seems like we ought to eat before we mix with any long yarns!"

So Case and Alex. took to the cabin, and the odors of steak and coffee and roasting duck soon filled the boat. While the good things were cooking the Rambler dropped down to a wharf where a tank wagon of gasoline awaited them, and there, also, loads of provisions of all kinds were put on board.

And the strangest part of it all was that there was nothing to pay! Red appeared to have temporary charge of the boat, and the bills seemed to have all been paid in advance. They were headed down stream when breakfast was eaten.

"We ought to reach the Gulf in three or four weeks, if we hurry!" Red observed, as he carved the ducks. "That is, if we hurry in the right way!"

"I thought it would take until spring," Chet broke in. "I hoped so!"

Alex. regarded the two with a whimsical smile on his freckled face.

"How long will it be before you'll both disappear?" he asked.

"Never again!" laughed Chet. "Say, boys, I did make a quick get-away a couple of times? What? I hated to go, but I just had to."

"Yes, and you prevented Case and I making one at the house in the city," Alex. said.

"It is all as simple as twice two," Red observed, sitting back from the table. "The robbery at Rock Island was planned and carried out by Sam, the outlaw who assisted me in the capture of the Rambler. I knew that at the time I was with him—at the time I let him go—or when you boys did, rather."

"But why didn't you pinch him?" demanded Alex. "There's a reward."

"Because I hadn't then discovered the goods which had been taken. He was going to take me to them, I being a possible purchaser!"

"Well, of all the nerve!" Jule cut in. "Just think of that, now!"

"Were they in that old house on the bayou?" asked Alex.

"Some of them were. As soon as I got off your boat I wired back to have the place surrounded and searched. They found all the silks and furs there! You boys did a good job for me when you permitted yourselves to be trapped."

"It was Captain Joe and Mose who did the good job when they got us out!" Jule said.

"Did you find Sam again?" asked Case, in a moment. "He was a corker!"

"You boys found him in the swamp," Red replied soberly, "and Mose executed the sentence of the law upon him — hanged him by the neck!"

"So you are a detective?" asked Case. "Why didn't you say so?"

"I am not," was the reply. "I am the owner of the warehouse that was robbed, and I set out to get the goods back, that is all."

"But you asked us to take Chet on down the river when he had the diamonds in his clothes!" Alex. exclaimed. "What about that? It was a funny stunt."

"Of course I didn't know that he had the diamonds," added Red, now to be known as Mr. George Redmond. "He told me about his having had them when I told him that Sam was dead, that was last night, in New Orleans. Then he told me that he had taken the diamonds from Sam because he wanted to restore them to me, but had promised Sam that he would never reveal his, Sam's, connection with the crime. Of course Sam never knew positively that the boy had stolen the diamonds, but he suspected."

"And sent this riverman, Gid Brent, on board at Cairo to see if the boy was there?"

"Yes, he did that. By that time I was satisfied that the boy had been in on the robbery — that he had been forced to enter the building by way of a window and open the door for the thieves to enter.

"I knew that the boy would tell the whole story to me if I could get him away from the robbers, and not scare him half to death by putting him in jail. So I followed him along down the river. As the robbers were making their way down toward New Orleans, too, I was doing a pretty good job following him — and especially as the robbers were after him, too. They believed, all but Sam, he had taken the diamonds, you see.

"They got him last night and searched him, but found nothing. Then they told him that if he would get Alex. and Case into their hands they would let him go. So Chet did that very thing, and now the two boys are witnesses that the robbers admitted to them that they were in on the robbery!

"When they let Chet go he made for the Rambler on a run, and found me on the way. All the people who were in the old house are under arrest. And the diamonds are up at Memphis in the deposit vault, and all is well."

"How do you know that?" demanded Clay.

"Why, we opened the box, the cashier and I," was the reply. "I knew they were there before I knew that Chet had ever had them. My one great difficulty was to get hold of the boy after he ran off at Memphis! Your boat was watched all the way down, you know, of course."

Then Clay told of his talk with the sheriff, and they all laughed at the idea that they had not seen through it all long before.

"If Chet had kept to boats I could have found him," Red went on, "but he rode on wreckage, and that made it difficult. I might have saved you boys and Chet some of this mystery talk if I had told you about it when I had Alex. in the cabin of my boat, after I knew where the diamonds were, but I thought I would let it work out for itself, especially as I was having the time of my life."

"I suppose those three mechanics were detectives, too?" asked Case.

"They were just what they represented themselves to be," was the reply, "and they got good positions at Vicksburg. They are expecting to meet you down the river, in a houseboat of their own. I saw them soon after they left you."

"I don't wonder the robbers wanted to get hold of Chet," laughed Alex. "They must have been red-headed when they found that the diamonds had been stolen from them!"

"Yes, they were," replied Chet, "but they didn't suspect me, at first. The man Brent, who came on board the Rambler at Cairo, would have killed me had he found me there. I was afraid he would, so I took to the river."

"And you took to the river again the night you threw the bag back on deck, too."

"Yes, I got pretty cold, too. I knew where the bag was, in the cabin, all the time, and I thought the diamonds were in it. Believing it would be safe, I did not take it and run away, as I had threatened to do, but when the cashier and another came on the boat I did take it and skip. When I found that the diamonds were not there I threw the bag back just to let you know I was wise to the game," he added.

"It is a commonplace story, after all, when you come to get it all told," said Mr. Redmond. "If it has spoiled your river trip I'm sorry for it!"

"We wouldn't have had any fun only for that!" cried Alex.

"Well," Clay cut in, "now we'll go down the river and have fun! We'll spend two months or more on the way to the Gulf, and then we'll put the motor boat on board a ship and sail her around to some point where we can get into the St. Lawrence river. The St. Lawrence comes next, you know."

"Why not put her on a gondola car again and take her as near to the headwaters of the St. Lawrence as we can?" asked Case. "I'd rather float down than sail up, any day."

"We will decide that when we get done here," Clay answered.

Those were two golden months for the boys, and Mr. Redmond seemed to enjoy the outing fully as much as any of them. They fished and hunted and loafed in the numerous passages of the delta of the Mississippi, and built roaring fires on the knolls, when they found them, and lived the care-free lives boys enjoy so much.

And then they were off for Chicago, and from there to the headwaters of the St. Lawrence. Their adventures on this noble river will be found in the next volume of this series; entitled:

"The Six River Motor Boys on the St. Lawrence; or, the Lost Channel."

Milton Keynes UK
Ingram Content Group UK Ltd.
UKHW010625250923
429338UK00004B/327

9 791041 952472